BOOK THREE
ENEMY LINES

C. Alexander London

SCHOLASTIC INC.

Copyright © 2015 by C. Alexander London

All rights reserved. Published by Scholastic Inc., *Publishers since 1920*. SCHOLASTIC and associated logos are trademarks and/or registered trademarks of Scholastic Inc.

The publisher does not have any control over and does not assume any responsibility for author or third-party websites or their content.

ISBN 978-0-545-80076-1

10 9 8 7 6 5 4 3 2 1   15 16 17 18 19/0

Printed in the U.S.A   40
First printing 2015

Book design by Sharismar Rodriguez & Carol Ly

For all those who serve others

PROLOGUE

CHIEF Petty Officer Cory McNab kept his finger on the trigger as he pressed his body flat against the side of a rusty forklift. He closed his eyes and held his breath, listening for the sound of gunfire.

His SIG SAUER P226N pistol had a silencer on it, but the rebel commandos hunting him had loud Kalashnikov rifles that would pop like firecrackers if they started shooting. He wondered if he'd hear the bullet coming. He wondered if he'd get a shot off before they found him.

They hadn't found him yet.

He heard only the gentle lapping of water against the dock. No gunshots, no alarms, no footfalls. The commandos didn't know he was here, on their base, in their territory, in the middle of the night.

If they found him, if he was caught, it would be an epic disaster — not just for him, not just for the members of the Navy's SEAL Team Five who had deployed with him, but for the United States of America itself. He was a chief petty officer assigned to the Navy's Special Forces command, and he was armed in a foreign country on a lethal mission that was supposed to remain top secret. If he was caught, the president of the United States would have a lot of explaining to do. The United States was not supposed to have soldiers here.

Cory felt like he was balanced on a razor's edge, the sharpest line between success and failure. He didn't want to stay out on this pier any longer than he had to. Every second of this mission was riskier than the seconds that came before it.

Over his shoulder, he looked at the recon squad of

Navy SEALs who were following his lead. Each of them gripped a silenced MP5 submachine gun as pitch-black as their wet suits. The SEALs were trained to operate on Sea, Air, and Land — any environment where their lethal skills were needed. Cory was not a SEAL, but he trusted them with his life. At this point in the mission, they were his only line of defense against an entire naval base of hostile enemy combatants. Although the lieutenant at his side outranked him, he would do whatever Cory needed him to.

This was Cory's mission, and the SEALs were waiting for him to move.

Another squad of SEALs floated offshore in a small black, inflatable boat, half a mile away. Their sniper would be scanning the dark pier through his magnifying scope, ready to provide cover and extraction if Cory's group needed to make an exit under enemy fire.

Of course, if they were under enemy fire, something had gone terribly wrong.

"Yo, Chief," the lieutenant beside him whispered. "You can't shoot with your eyes closed. Open up."

Cory was glad for the cover of night and the black smudge on his face. The SEALs couldn't see him blush.

He opened his eyes and lowered his weapon, slipping it back into his leg holster. He wasn't much of a marksman, anyway. That wasn't why he was with this team. He touched the padded pocket of his vest, making sure the syringe was secure, along with the compressed-air cartridge that was meant to deliver the syringe's payload: a dose of lethal poison.. *That's* why he was on this mission. All he had to do was locate his target, inject him with the poison dart, and then he and the SEALs could all go home, mission accomplished.

He pointed to his eyes, then around the corner, telling the rest of the team he was going to have a look.

The coast was clear. A blanket of mist rose from the surface of the water, shrouding the pier in a gloomy haze. Floodlights ran along the fence that separated it from the rest of the naval complex, once shared peacefully between Ukrainian and Russian forces, now in the hands of Russian separatist commandos. It had been a bold move, and while world leaders debated what to do about it, Cory and his team were taking action.

He hoped they didn't have to enter the buildings beyond the fences. There would be more guards, and if those guards saw them they would have to be eliminated in silence. He didn't want anyone else to die on this mission, not even the enemy. They weren't *his* enemy, after all. This might be his mission, but it was not his war.

He hadn't even wanted this mission in the first place.

But Cory was the most senior member of the dolphin-handler squad, and it was his responsibility to do the dirty work that lie ahead. Like it or not, this was all up to him.

He chased his doubts away, and his fears, and he moved quickly from behind the cover of the forklift, crouching low, stepping silently along the pier. His wet suit was rapidly cooling in the night air, and a chill went through his body. The lightweight breathing apparatus on his back felt suddenly heavier, and all the scuba equipment he wore weighed him down. He was in good shape, but hardly as good as the Navy SEALs, who trained year-round to run, crawl, swim, and fight in this heavy, wet gear.

He didn't have to go far, though, before he saw what he was looking for. About one hundred feet ahead, there was a fenced-off area, where the wood planks of the pier formed a square — a protected area of water. The area was ringed with razor-wire fencing and a secure metal door. Under the surface, there would be netting to separate the square underwater pen from the rest of the Black Sea. It was meant to keep unwanted sea creatures out. And keep one specific sea creature in.

That pen was where he needed to be.

Cory gestured for a SEAL to follow, then he slipped into the water, lowering himself in slowly so that he didn't make a sound. He put the regulator in his mouth and ducked below the surface, then kicked forward, swimming fast and silent.

He glided beneath the dock and, in a few strokes, arrived at the underwater netting of the sea pen. One of the SEALs was already at his side. He didn't know the man's name, rating, or call sign. Other than the lieutenant, he didn't know any of the SEALs. And they didn't really know him. All the same, they watched his back. The other two had stayed on the surface to cover the underwater team while they worked.

The SEAL with Cory used wire cutters to snip open a small hole in the netting, just big enough for a person to squeeze through. Cory removed the syringe from his vest and attached it to the cartridge. The sharp dart on the end would puncture the skin, and the gas in the cartridge would inject the syringe's fluid with enough force to penetrate even the toughest layers of flesh.

He breathed in, listening to the hiss of air from his tank, and exhaled again. The apparatus didn't let any bubbles escape; it was a stealth diving rig.

He swam through the opening, needle dart up and ready. He tried to stay calm, keep his eyes open in the dark water. He couldn't see. Murky shapes seemed to slice the water, just at the edge of his sight, vanishing if he tried to look at them directly.

He snapped down his night-vision scope, and the watery world turned acid green in his goggles. He saw the base of the pier's support pillars crusted with algae. He saw the outline of the underwater netting, hanging from strong hooks off the underside of the dock. He saw the glow of the surface lights above.

And straight ahead, he saw a six-hundred-pound Atlantic bottlenose dolphin, eyes bright with curiosity, jaw bent into a big dolphin smile.

Cory was a trained dolphin handler, a lover of these brilliant sea mammals, and he considered himself a friend to all dolphins. He liked how they were perfectly designed for the lives they led, never seeming out of place in their strange ocean realm. He liked how they didn't judge, and he liked how they didn't hold grudges.

Often, Cory thought he preferred dolphins to people.

But he wasn't here to make friends with a dolphin.

This dolphin was the target . . . and Cory was the assassin.

He braced himself as, with a flick of its tail, the long, gray dolphin charged.

01:

TOP-SECRET SYSTEMS

FOUR DAYS EARLIER

IT had been the driest February anyone could remember at Naval Base Point Loma in San Diego. All of California had been suffering a drought, even though winter was supposed to be a rainy time. Farmers were nervous for their crops failing. Firemen were nervous about wildfires spreading in the dry brush, and the city of San Diego itself was starting to plan for a summer of water rationing.

Cory McNab, however, was as wet as ever.

He spent most of his days in the water, training with Kaj, an Atlantic bottlenose dolphin, whom he considered his partner in the United States Navy Marine Mammal Program.

Kaj was one of the most well-trained dolphins the navy had ever employed. He'd been born in an aquarium in Baltimore and moved to the navy's research station when he was very young. He'd trained with sailors and doctors and marine biologists. He'd deployed around the world on military exercises, some of them top secret, and he'd been rewarded with a kind of retirement and all the fresh fish he could eat. He was a research and training dolphin now.

Kaj and Cory would demonstrate techniques to the other handlers and trainers in the program, but the navy was more interested in studying Kaj's abilities than using them in the field. The most common work of the navy's dolphin teams — locating military equipment on the ocean floor, guarding the ships in port against illegal swimmers in the water, or searching for undersea explosive mines in dangerous waters all over the globe — that was now the work of the less-experienced dolphins.

There were three dozen other trainers and handlers at their base, along with several civilian technicians, assistants, veterinarians, researchers, and students, who studied all the amazing things the dolphins could do. Since the program's beginning in 1960, over eight hundred research papers about dolphins and other marine mammals had been published based on the work of the Marine Mammal Program. The core of their mission, however, still boiled down to a simple idea: a dolphin and the dolphin's human handler working together to protect the navy's fleet. Everything revolved around that team of two.

Each of the dolphin teams was organized into a group called a *system*. Some of the systems focused only on finding explosives buried on the ocean floor, others specialized in finding explosives that floated in the middle of the ocean, while still others guarded ports or recovered special equipment that had been dropped or hidden in the ocean.

The most elite of the dolphins and their handlers could do all these things and more, and it was Cory's job — along with Kaj — to identify and train the best of the best to join a squad known by the mysterious name MK 6D, which they pronounced *Mark Sixty*. Officially, the Mark Sixty system did not exist. It was classified top secret, even though the rest of the navy's Marine Mammal Program had been declassified twenty years ago.

As far as most people knew, the Navy Marine Mammal Program only had five Marine Mammal Systems. MK 6D was never discussed openly. The few dolphin teams who were chosen to be a part of it could do the things no other individual team could do. They could move faster and accomplish more than any other Marine Mammal team in the navy's arsenal. The navy considered them essential defensive weapons and expected them to be ready to deploy anywhere they were needed around the world within seventy-two hours of receiving an order.

Except they hadn't received an order to deploy in the entire time Cory had been training them. They were new, and no one knew quite what was expected of them.

At the moment, the world didn't seem to need the help of a covert dolphin force. The regular dolphin systems could guard the ports, and the regular Special Forces could do the fighting on land that the United States military required. Cory sometimes questioned the point of building his new Special Forces–dolphin hybrid system. There was even talk about retiring all of the dolphins in the navy and replacing them with robots within a couple of years.

But until that happened, Cory had to keep doing his job.

At that moment, there were three dolphin-and-human-partner teams that Cory had assigned to MK 6D, and one other team that showed promise if they kept working at it.

"You need to focus on the clarity of your movements," Cory explained to the dolphin handler, a young guy they called *Skunk* because he had a white streak in his short brown hair, like the fur of a skunk's back. Even after Skunk had shaved his head, the streak was visible. His dolphin was named Tomas.

"Tomas knows what I want him to do," Skunk explained to Cory. "He's just being stubborn."

"Show me his water exit," Cory said, dangling his legs off the edge of the pier. He slapped the surface, calling Kaj over. Kaj bumped Cory's feet with his snout and rolled over onto his back so that Cory could rub his belly under his front flippers, which was Kaj's second-favorite thing. His favorite was to have his tongue scratched. Cory saved tongue scratching for special rewards.

Skunk stood up from the pier and walked over to the sea pen, where Tomas was swimming in circles. Skunk bent down and slapped the surface of the water, just like Cory had, which got Tomas's attention. The dolphin's head popped up from the water, his small black eyes shining as he looked to his handler, awaiting a command. A technician watched from the other side, clipboard in hand. Skunk glanced nervously at the technician and at Cory, then down to Tomas.

"Here we go, Mister T," he whispered, then made a big gesture with his hand and his arm, sweeping from the water to the pier.

Tomas immediately dove underwater, his sleek silver body shooting like lighting just under the surface as he sped to the pier, jumped from the water, and slid on his belly along the dock. His back was arched, his head lifted so he didn't bump his snout, and his tail raised like the foil on the back of a race car.

However, he was moving too fast and there was a mischievous glint to his shining black eyes. As he slid, he turned his tail slightly, sweeping Skunk's feet out from under him. The dolphin kept sliding across the pier, right off the other side and back into the water, and Skunk fell backward and splashed, fully clothed, into the water behind him.

Cory blew his whistle, and Tomas swam underneath the pier and popped up by his side. Skunk hauled himself out of the water and stood, his blue utilities dripping, next to Cory. Tomas used a flick of his head to splash water onto his handler, showing that he'd just been playing around. Skunk frowned.

Cory laughed. "That's not quite the move," he told the young dolphin handler. "Ideally, the dolphin exits the water and stops . . . and doesn't knock you in after him."

"I know it!" said Skunk. "And so does he! I swear, it's just that he likes to play around too much. I can do better."

"You'll have to," Cory told him, the smile vanishing from his face. "If you want to be on my team, you've got to let your partner know when playtime's over. When you're on a boat moving in the ocean, and you need your dolphin aboard, he can't go sliding back off again. If he thinks it's playtime in a combat situation, it could be lights-out for you, for him, and for the mission."

Skunk nodded. "Mm-hmm," he said. Cory noticed he was now fighting back a laugh, looking right over Cory's shoulder.

Cory turned and saw his own dolphin using his tail to rise most of the way out of the water, almost like he was standing, and wiggling his body so he moved backward, "moonwalking."

Cory blew his whistle, and Kaj swam over to him, mouth open for a tongue scratching.

"No way, buddy," he told his dolphin. "You just made me look bad!"

Kaj just stared up at him, openmouthed, and Cory found his resolve melting away. He bent down and scratched his dolphin's tongue.

"Okay, Skunk," he said over his shoulder. "Let's take a break. Sometimes, it *is* up to the dolphins when playtime's over. And I guess it's not over yet."

02:
PLAYTIME'S END

A FEW minutes later, Cory and Skunk stood beside another dolphin's pen, watching Special Warfare Boat Operator Petty Officer First Class Preeti Suraj — SB-1 in the abbreviated way navy-enlisted sailors were identified — whose dolphin, Kojak, had been one of the first to join the new team under Cory's leadership.

"You could learn something from SB-1 Suraj," Cory told Skunk. "See how clear her movements are? Using unclear movements to communicate with your dolphin is like mumbling when you're talking to someone.

It's no good giving instructions if they can't be understood."

"So you want me to be more like Suraj?" Skunk asked.

"I do," Cory told him.

Although, really, he wasn't sure he did want Skunk to be more like her. She was the best he had on his team, but she wasn't much fun to work with.

Preeti Suraj had been one of the first women ever admitted to the Navy's Special Warfare Combatant-craft Crewman program, where she'd trained to crew boats on some of the most dangerous missions in the world, inserting and extracting Navy SEALs for their missions, sometimes under enemy fire.

Although she'd graduated from the training, there'd been controversy over her deployment in a unit of all men, and she was transferred to Cory's dolphin program. Since arriving, she'd worked harder than anyone, determined to prove she would not be slowed down by the transfer. She had ambition. She was all business and tough as nails. To prove she belonged among the most elite combat soldiers in the world, she had striven to be twice as good as the men she had trained alongside, and she brought that same attitude to the dolphin program.

In truth, she intimidated Cory.

He had dropped out of the Navy SEAL training program years ago, and even though he'd served in combat himself and was her supervisor in the dolphin program, he wondered if she actually respected him. She could break him in half if she wanted to.

With a sharp move of her arm, she signaled to her dolphin, Kojak, to leap from the water and slide to a stop, perfectly still, in front of her. Then, with another gesture, Kojak rolled himself back into the water, vanishing below the surface without a sound and hardly a splash. A moment later, the dolphin was back, eyes bright, waiting for his next instruction. Preeti tossed him a fish and signaled that he could relax, and the dolphin swam off to trace lazy circles in the water around the training area. Even her dolphin's playtime seemed more serious than the others'.

"I'm trying to be more like her, Chief," Skunk said. "I can't help that Tomas likes to goof off more than Kojak does."

"No use blaming the faults of the handler on the dolphin," Preeti told him. "You want to be on this team, you don't make excuses."

"I'll give the pep talks around here," Cory told her. She gave him a withering stare, then returned her attention to her dolphin, slapping the surface, so that Kojak came straight over to get back to work. The moment Kojak reappeared in the water at her feet, she bent down to scratch the appreciative dolphin's tongue and whisper sweet words that only her aquatic partner could hear. It was amazing to see how someone so tough could be so gentle with the animal in her care.

Cory turned his own attention back to Skunk. "Why don't you and Tomas practice for a few more minutes before I send the interns down to clean up? You've got another evaluation next week, and if I can't pass you, we've got to reassign you guys to one of the other dolphin systems. Mark Sixty qualification demands at least a ninety-five percent score on every skill. So work on your water exit and return."

"Aye aye, Chief," Skunk said, but his mouth turned down as he said it. He was already trying as hard as he thought he could, and he still wasn't making the grade. The test he had to pass next week would take only a few hours, but it would determine the rest of his career. The guy had a lot riding on how quickly Tomas learned.

Skunk's test results would also be recorded in Cory's file. If he failed to train up enough people, he surely wouldn't be allowed to keep running this program for long. He wanted Skunk to pass because he liked Skunk, but he also needed Skunk to pass because he needed *someone* to pass.

Cory returned to Kaj to show one more demonstration of the perfect exit and return to the water. It wasn't exactly necessary to show Skunk again, but he wanted to prove that he was still as good as Preeti. One thing about having a reputation as the best was that there was always someone coming up who was trying to be better. Cory wasn't sure why he felt her opinion of him as a dolphin handler mattered so much, but he couldn't help it. He noticed her watching him with Kaj and he gave her a respectful nod. She gave him one back and returned to her work.

Skunk kept practicing, and Cory left to go back to his office. He stopped short, however, when he saw the dolphin program's commanding officer, Commander Jackson, strolling toward him down the pier, her white uniform blindingly bright in the afternoon sun. Beside her, walking in lockstep, were two square-jawed officers that Cory didn't recognize, a lieutenant junior grade and a lieutenant commander. He gave them both a salute.

"Chief McNab," Commander Jackson said. "Is your team deployment ready?"

"Yes, ma'am," Cory told her, puzzled. She knew they were always supposed to be deployment ready. That was why they trained all the time. To stay ready.

"And yourself?" she added. "You and your *system*?"

She used the word *system* instead of saying *dolphin* or even saying Kaj's name, which made Cory suspicious. She certainly knew his name.

"Kaj is retired from deployment, ma'am," he reminded her.

"He has just been reactivated," the lieutenant commander told Cory severely. Cory saw that both he and the lieutenant junior grade beside him wore the Special Warfare Operator Badge on their uniforms. They were both Navy SEALs.

"Respectfully, sir," Cory responded, trying to sound confident although his throat had suddenly gone dry, "the deployment readiness of my dolphins is my determination." He thought his heart might beat its way out of his chest, it was thumping so fast. It was not wise to argue with a superior officer, especially one he didn't know. *Especially* one with Special Forces insignia on his uniform.

But Kaj had served his country more than any dolphin should have to, and Cory would not be responsible for putting him in danger again.

Commander Jackson, however, gave Cory a look like a hurricane, and he clamped his mouth shut.

"Your commander will brief you," the senior officer said, then turned on his heels and walked away down the pier, the other man at his side.

Once they were out of earshot, Cory shook his head and asked Commander Jackson, "Ma'am, what was that all about?"

The commander sighed. "You need to get out of the water sometimes and watch the news," she told Cory. She pulled a newspaper out of the folder she'd been carrying and handed it to him.

Cory looked down and saw the headline.

RUSSIAN SEPARATISTS SEIZE CRIMEA

"Yesterday, intelligence confirmed that Russian troops fanned out from the naval base at Sevastopol and seized the Crimean peninsula from the nation of Ukraine," the commander explained.

"Okay?" said Cory, not yet sure what that had to do with him or the dolphin program. He didn't even know where Crimea was in the world.

"There are two Ukrainian warships trapped, just outside that naval base, on the Black Sea," Commander Jackson continued. "Our dolphins are the only ones who can locate undersea mines and secure passage from the base quickly and safely before the Russian commandos decide to seize those ships for themselves and set off a full-scale war in the region."

"So it's mine clearance that we need to do?" Cory asked. "You don't need Mark Sixty for that. One of the other dolphin teams can certainly handle it."

Commander Jackson shook her head. "That Russian naval base on the Black Sea is also the site of the Russian dolphin program," she added. "And we have reason to believe their dolphins are trained for use as offensive weapons."

"You mean —?" Cory began.

"The Russians may have trained their dolphins to kill," she said. "We don't know. We don't know how many dolphins they have or if they have *any* dolphins anymore. Our intelligence on that base is sketchy. But one way or another, you and your team are going to find out."

Cory stared at the newspaper in his hand. There was a picture of a group of Russian commandos in uniforms without any markings on them, taking down a Ukrainian flag from a government building that they'd seized.

"There will be a briefing at eighteen hundred," Commander Jackson told him. "Have your whole team there. Including the new one, EOD-3 Reggerio."

"Skunk?" Cory said, using the nickname instead of the formal description of Charlie Reggerio, a petty officer third class rated as an Explosive Ordnance Disposal Technician. It was so much easier just to call him *Skunk*. "He's not on the team yet. I don't think he's ready."

"He's just been made ready," said Commander Jackson. "Understood?"

"Yes, ma'am," said Cory, giving her a salute, which she returned, then left him standing alone on the pier, his pants still dripping wet where he'd been dangling them in the water.

Her words rang through his head. *The Russians may have trained their dolphins to kill.*

He glanced back toward the dolphins and their handlers farther down the dock.

Kaj was happily mimicking all the training motions Tomas was going through in the water, opening his jaws wide each time to get a fish from Skunk, even though it wasn't his turn. Skunk, laughing, obeyed and tossed Kaj some of the fish meant for Tomas.

"Playtime's over," Cory said aloud to himself. His dolphins were going to war.

03:
DOLPHIN VERSUS DOLPHIN

THERE was a good reason Cory's dolphin team was top secret.

People like to think of dolphins as lovable sea creatures, intelligent and kindly beings who haunt the oceans like friendly ghosts. Their faces always hold a smile, and their squeaking language sounds like a song. Everybody loves stories about sailors saved from drowning or swimmers saved from shark attacks by pods of wild dolphins, the superheroes of the sea.

Cory himself had been saved from sharks *and* from drowning by dolphins. He even owed his life to Kaj, after a mission in North Korea had gone wrong.

But Cory knew that what people wanted to believe about dolphins and what was really true about dolphins were different matters entirely.

The famous dolphin smile was only an illusion brought on by the shape of their jaw. Their language of squeaks and clicks allowed them to hunt in packs underwater, coordinating their attacks on schools of fish. And dolphins were among the few animals on earth who didn't only kill for food or self-defense. Sometimes, dolphins had been known to kill sharks, porpoises, or even other, weaker dolphins just for sport.

In that way, Cory realized, they were terribly like humans.

Although humans were the only creatures on earth who waged war. Humans were the only creatures who formed armies and assigned generals to give orders for other humans to fight each other. Humans were also the only creatures who enlisted other animals in their wars, like cavalry horses, bomb-sniffing dogs, and dolphins.

Cory wasn't sure how he felt about using dolphins and sea lions for military purposes, the way the navy's

Marine Mammal Program did, and he had doubts about his own role in their use, training dolphin teams for the most perilous missions. The program had done a lot of good over the years — and not only by saving lives and protecting ships. The navy's research with the dolphins in their care helped scientists understand dolphin behavior and biology better than ever, which helped conservationists learn how best to protect them. In a way, the service of these dolphins in captivity protected dolphins in the wild, kind of like how the service of the men and women in the navy protected the civilians in the rest of America. Cory believed that to be true, but still . . . these dolphins hadn't volunteered to be in the military the way the humans had.

Somehow, in the months since he'd been promoted to lead the top-secret dolphin program, he hadn't thought much about the reality of what he was training his dolphin teams to do. He'd put his thoughts into different boxes: his love of the ocean and respect for sea creatures in one box, his job training dolphins to work with military Special Forces in the other. And then he kept those boxes shut tight.

But the new mission was about to rip those boxes right open, shake them up, and toss all the contents together.

"As you are now aware," one of the square-jawed officers told Cory as he sat in the front row of a fluorescent-lit briefing room, "Russian Special Forces are operating on the Crimean peninsula on the Black Sea in what the US unofficially believes is an illegal annexation of Ukrainian territory."

"What's he talking about?" Skunk leaned over to whisper in Cory's ear. The air smelled heavily of chlorine and salt water from the dolphin trainers on the folding chairs around Cory.

Preeti had her notebook in hand, jotting down important details from the briefing. The other handlers on his team, Petty Officer Second Class Ramon Cruz and Petty Officer Second Class Greg Tully also had their notebooks out. Petty Officer Third Class Charlie Reggerio — Skunk — did not have his notebook out. He didn't even seem to have a notebook with him. He drummed his fingers on his thighs and looked out of his depth, totally confused, but also terribly excited.

His eyes drank in the uniform of the Special Forces lieutenant commander who was briefing them and the slide show projected on the screen behind him. He looked at the other dolphin handlers and at the coffeepot in the corner and even up at the dull ceiling tiles. It was like he was trying to memorize every detail of the room, with no idea what was actually worth paying attention to. Cory thought of him like a junior-varsity quarterback suddenly called up to play in the NFL. He wasn't ready, and both he and Cory knew it.

But it was Cory's job to get him ready.

"Reggerio!" Commander Jackson snapped from the corner of the room where she stood watching the briefing alongside the lieutenant junior grade. "What could possibly be so important that you feel the need to whisper during the commander's briefing?"

"Ma'am, I was just asking for clarification," Skunk

answered. "About the . . . er, uh . . . Crimea? Like, what's it matter to us?"

Commander Jackson looked like she was about to snap Skunk's head off and feed it to the dolphins outside, but the commander in the front of the room spoke first.

"The Crimean peninsula is Ukrainian territory that Russia has long sought to claim as its own," he said. "They have finally acted on that claim and have sent troops to support a group of rebel separatists, trying to take the territory for themselves. In short, Russia has invaded and taken over a part of another country. From the naval base they control on the Black Sea, they will be able to menace the entire region, threatening to seize more territory, more natural resources, and shift the entire balance of power in that part of the world in their favor."

"But, sir, respectfully?" Skunk called out, his voice wavering just slightly. "So what?"

Cory tensed. He fought the urge to jab Skunk in the ribs. This lieutenant commander was a battle-hardened officer, not someone to be joked with, needled, or pressed to explain himself. Cory had never really insisted on much discipline from his team, seeing as they spent most of their time cleaning up fish guts and doing paperwork, but now he felt responsible for Skunk's insouciance, a word which he'd never had a reason to use before. It meant a boyish lack of respect, an indifference to authority, and it made the whole MK 6D system look bad.

The lieutenant commander, however, didn't appear fazed.

"The reasons that we don't want to see Russian power grow in the region are not your concern, EOD Reggerio," the commander told him. "Why don't we let the president worry about that? Your concern, at this moment, is to deploy to our ship in the Black Sea." He cleared his throat and changed the slide from a map of Crimea to a map of the Black Sea, with areas highlighted for the American ship, the Russian naval base, and the two Ukranian warships stuck in the harbor. "Officially, of course, Russia denies having sent soldiers to assist the separatist commandos taking over Crimea, and likewise, *officially*, the United States is not involved, either."

Cory shifted in his seat. This was the way modern wars were fought, in secret, with public statements by politicians that hid the truth of what soldiers on the ground were doing. If their mission failed, it would be a disaster because the lies would crumble apart. If they succeeded, no one would ever know. That was how covert operations worked. There were no victory parades.

"Once in the area of operations," the commander continued, "your dolphin systems will enter the harbor at Sevastopol with members of the Explosive Ordnance Disposal unit and operators from SEAL Team Five, who will provide security as you clear the area of undersea mines and prevent harassment of the Ukrainian warships by Russian forces. Once the Ukrainian ships are safely out of danger, you will return to the fleet for further orders as needed. That is your mission. That is *all* you need to know. Understood?"

"Yes, sir," said Skunk, whose ears had turned red, but who kept his cheeks from blushing at least.

"From now on, keep your mouth shut," Cory whispered to him. Skunk nodded.

"Sir?" Preeti raised her hand. "Will we be discussing rules of engagement?"

The ghost of a smile passed over the commander's face, but he kept his composure. "The SEAL Team will be thoroughly prepared to repel any danger to your systems," he said. "It is our hope to avoid escalating an already tense situation. We do not want to enter into open conflict with the separatist commandos or the Russian military. You are, however, authorized to protect your dolphins and each other. Further instructions will come from the mission commanders on site. Operational control will be up to the Mark Sixty Team."

Preeti glanced at Cory. Once they were overseas, he'd be in charge of their covert mission. He couldn't tell if she was happy about that or not.

Commander Jackson stepped to the front of the briefing room. "This is what you've trained for," she told them all. "Your dolphins know how to find and tag undersea mines. Do that quickly and quietly, and those Ukrainian ships can get out of port. We are trying to stop a war, not start one. That said . . ." She paused and locked eyes with Cory. "You should all know that the Russians have their own dolphin program at the naval base where you will be operating. We don't know how many dolphins they have, but we believe that they have trained dolphins in swimmer nullification."

Skunk shifted in his seat, fighting the urge to speak, but the confusion on his face was obvious enough.

"Swimmer nullification," Commander Jackson explained without being asked, "is the use of dolphins to attack swimmers, divers, and other assets with lethal force. The dolphins are equipped with needles on the end of their snouts. These needles are attached to high-pressure cartridges so that when the dolphin rams its target with the needle, a burst of carbon dioxide is injected into the bloodstream. This both forces the diver to the surface and, as the gas expands, causes lethal embolism."

Every trainer in the room tensed, even Skunk, who was well trained enough as a scuba diver to understand what this meant. The Russian dolphins could inject a swimmer with gas that would expand rapidly and cause the diver to literally blow up. The Swimmer Nullification Program had been rumored for years, but no one had ever confirmed its existence until now.

"The SEALs will be watching your back while you locate the mines, but we need you, in turn, to watch theirs. Use what you know about dolphin behavior. Observe, and if necessary, *act* to protect the mission. Understood?"

"Aye aye!" they all responded in unison, although they couldn't possibly know what she meant by "act to protect the mission." No one could know. That was why they had been chosen to deploy. Cory's team was better suited to handle surprises than any other dolphin team. He really hoped they wouldn't run into any.

"You're expected aboard ship in the Black Sea seventy-two hours from now," said Commander Jackson. "Let's get to it. Dismissed."

Cory's team stood from their chairs as the officers left the room. The trainers all looked to Cory, somewhat shocked. It was safe to say that none of them ever expected to go up against a pod of enemy dolphins in hostile territory in some foreign sea. It was safe to say Cory himself never expected it, either. This mission would put them and their dolphins directly in harm's way. Perhaps Skunk was right to ask why, but no answer could possibly satisfy any of them. Their job was not to question why, theirs was just to do or . . . He didn't let himself finish the rhyme "to do or die."

Better just to focus on the job, one step at a time. Their first step was certainly a complicated one. They had to get five dolphins out of the ocean, onto airplanes, over to the other side of the world, and onto a naval ship at sea in three days. There was little room for error when transporting a six-hundred-pound dolphin, let alone five of them, and Cory knew from experience that dolphins did not especially like to fly. The strain of air travel alone could kill a dolphin before it ever got to its mission.

The moment Cory's team stepped back outside, the clock was ticking, and every decision he made from that point on was a matter of life or death.

04:
MOVING FISH

OUTSIDE, the afternoon sun glinted off the Pacific Ocean and it took a moment for Cory's eyes to adjust. He breathed the salty air in deep, and exhaled slowly, thinking through all the things that needed to be done, for the dolphins and for himself. He'd have to pack. He'd have to let his roommate and his family know he was shipping out. He'd have to explain to them why he was shipping out, when he'd told them before that he would never be sent on a mission like this again. He'd thought his top-secret mission days were done.

But the United States Navy had other plans for him.

As he walked out, he sent his little brother, Aaron, a text to call him back, then he dropped his phone in his pocket and turned his attention to the job ahead.

Time to get the team moving.

He ordered Preeti to meet with the veterinarians and tell them to prepare for deployment. He sent Tully to set up the mobile harnesses and told Cruz to start talking to the technicians about what would happen over the next twenty-four hours. They all had a deployment checklist and it was time to go through it point by point. There would be no missteps, no cut corners, and no details left to chance.

"We do everything by the book and we'll get this done without a problem," he told them. "Don't forget we have *two* missions here — the mission we've been assigned and the mission to care for and protect our dolphins, understood?"

"Aye aye," said his handlers, and they all snapped to it. Only Skunk lingered behind, unsure of what to do next.

"Skunk, welcome to the team. Mark Sixty is glad to have you." Skunk smiled warily, his face pale and his eyes as wide as oceans.

Cory knew what it felt like to think you didn't belong. Dolphin teams had never deployed with Special Forces until he and Kaj had come along, and he'd always felt like an outsider. When he first started, he knew the Navy SEALs hadn't wanted him around, which made him work that much harder to prove himself. Now he was the leader of his own Special Forces team and there was someone new in his place: practically a kid, like Cory had been, and he was just as terrified as Cory had been, too. Skunk was trying not to show it, but Cory knew the signs all too well: Skunk was going to freak out.

Cory didn't want to overwhelm the youngest and newest member of the team right away, so he decided to give him one of the easier jobs, although it was also one of the most important.

"How much does Tomas eat in a day?" he asked.

Skunk cocked his head at him, surprised by the pop quiz. "Uh . . . about thirty-six pounds of fish."

"Correct," said Cory. "And Kaj?"

"The same," said Skunk. He recited some of what he'd learned in training. "Atlantic bottlenose dolphins consume roughly six percent of their body weight every day."

"And how many dolphins are we deploying?"

"Four?" said Skunk.

"Five," corrected Cory. "Kaj and I are coming, too."

"Five, then."

"Very good," said Cory. "How'd you do in math in high school?"

"I . . . uh, well . . . I wasn't, like, the best . . ." Skunk didn't know how to answer or why he was being asked such strange questions, which was just what Cory wanted. He had to keep Skunk's mind focused and busy and not worrying about dangers he couldn't predict. Hard work was the best antidote to fear.

"I'm going to need you to start doing the math to secure our order of restaurant-quality mackerel for the deployment," Cory told him. "We're going to need a lot of fish."

"How long are we deploying for?" Skunk asked.

Cory paused. He didn't know, but he figured they should have plenty of fish on hand in case resupplying proved difficult. "Secure enough for seven days," he said.

"Aye aye," Skunk replied.

"And double-check your math before you place the order," Cory said. "The last thing you want to deal with is a dolphin who's missed snack time."

Skunk nodded and jogged off to get the paperwork together for ordering a huge quantity of fish. It was a little known fact that the navy's dolphins ate far better than the navy's humans. The dolphin program, even the top-secret team, had to follow all the laws and guidelines about housing and caring for dolphins, the same as public aquariums. Not only did their dolphins eat a lot of top-quality fish, but they traveled with a huge staff of veterinarians, trainers, assistants, and technicians whose sole job was to maintain the health and well-being of the animals.

Atlantic bottlenose dolphins are tough mammals, but they don't take well to air transport. They've evolved perfectly for their ocean environment. Their bodies are sleek and powerful so they can swim extremely fast; their echolocation allows them to hunt and communicate with each other over long distances below the surface; and even their hard snouts — called the *rostrum* — evolved to help them root around through the sand on the ocean floor. They can dive to depths that humans can only dream of without a submarine, and come back up again safely in a fraction of the time anything man-made could do. When necessary, a dolphin can stay underwater without breathing for nearly half an hour, but they prefer to surface more often. Normally, a dolphin comes to the surface to breathe through the blowhole on the top of its head a few times every minute, then dives below again to where they're most comfortable: under the water.

Moving a dolphin to the other side of the world, however, made them very uncomfortable, and that discomfort could cause them enormous stress. To get to the Black Sea, Cory's MK 6D dolphins would have to be out of the water for well over a full day. Because they were mammals and breathed air, they wouldn't suffocate like fish out of water, but keeping them cool, wet, and calm during travel was hard work.

Their dolphins were trained to jump into their harnesses, which were fleece-lined slings with straps to hold them securely in place. The slings were suspended above small tanks of water. The five dolphin harnesses and mobile tanks would be wheeled into the belly of a giant C-130 cargo plane, along with the rest of their supplies and their team. Then they would fly to an air base in Romania and take a series of trucks to the port, where they would load the dolphin harnesses into the belly of the US Navy Dock Landing Ship *McNamara*, where each dolphin would have his own inflatable pool to swim in until they reached the area of operations off the coast of Crimea.

During this whole long trip, the handler or an assistant would stay by each dolphin's side. They would dump water over the heads and bodies of the dolphins every few minutes and would rub their backs and scratch their tongues. They'd also brush their teeth, feed them fish, and help the veterinary technicians give them medical checkups every few hours.

Even with all these precautions, it could still be very dangerous for a dolphin to travel so far. The entire process was very confusing for them, and the stress could even be fatal. Cory imagined it somewhat like taking a human out of his home, shoving him into a tiny spaceship, and launching him into space without ever telling him where he was going or why. It'd be enough to give anyone a heart attack.

In its entire history, the navy's dolphin program had only suffered one dolphin casualty while on a mission. In 1987, a dolphin named Skippy had died of pneumonia in the Persian Gulf. Cory was determined not to break the twenty-seven-year streak. He would supervise everything.

He watched the flurry of activity on the pier carefully, looking over his own checklists as the support teams went through theirs. Nothing would be missed. Nothing would be forgotten. This wasn't training; this was what they all trained for. Even the dolphins seemed to know something was up.

They popped their heads from the water, watching the humans scurrying around above them. A veterinary technician was getting in the water with an intern to examine Tully's dolphin, Keanu. Cruz's dolphin, Zeus, watched the exam closely — the two dolphins were brothers and both had been born at the same research center. They always seemed to have a keen interest in what the other was up to. Tomas was playing with another intern, slapping the surface of the water, mimicking whatever the intern did.

Cory didn't see Kaj at first, then noticed his big gray partner floating just below the surface, his tail flicking ever so slightly every few seconds. He was barely moving and seemed to be watching everything going on in the water and on the pier all at once. When he saw Cory coming toward him, he swam over to the edge of the pier and popped his head out of the water, clicking from his blowhole in what Cory had come to realize was his own way of saying hello to his handler.

"Hey, pal," Cory said. He pulled on high rubber boots that rested in a bin of cleaning solution, and tucked his uniform's pant legs into the boots before dangling his feet into the water. It wasn't so much to keep his pants dry as to keep the water clean and free of anything from on land that could make the dolphins sick.

Kaj bumped Cory's legs with his body, asking for Cory to jump in and swim with him.

"No can do," Cory answered. "A little busy right now." He spoke as if Kaj could understand him, even though he was pretty sure that dolphins didn't actually understand English. They could learn a few words, but only simple commands over months of training.

Cory and Kaj had their own way of communicating, through gestures, sounds, and expressions, but it had very little to do with words. Sometimes Cory envied those ape researchers who could teach their gorillas sign language and engage them in conversation. Living in the water, what use would a dolphin have for conversation?

But still, Cory talked to Kaj. It made him feel better.

"Looks like we're coming out of retirement," he said, patting the dolphin just behind his blowhole. Kaj's skin was smooth, but tough. Dolphins could be pretty rough with each other, and their sharp teeth tore skin, even in play. They healed quickly, though, in a way scientists didn't fully understand yet. Cory imagined them a bit like Wolverine from the X-Men comics, who could heal miraculously fast. Dolphins were like the navy's X-Men. They could do things no human could, and many of their abilities remained mysterious. But like Wolverine, they could still be hurt. Most dolphins developed scars and scratches throughout their lives.

Cory traced his fingers along a deep scar that ran in an arc around Kaj's head from when he'd been trapped in the collapse of an underwater cave on their last mission. "I know it's not right," he said. "I know we made a deal that you'd never be sent on a military mission again . . . but things change. The navy doesn't make promises to dolphins, I guess."

"No, we don't," Commander Jackson said, startling him. He popped to his feet to salute her, splashing her crisp uniform in the process.

"Sorry, ma'am," Cory spluttered. "I just —"

"At ease, Sailor," Commander Jackson said. "I know you don't want this deployment."

Cory took a deep breath. He wasn't sure how much he should say to his superior officer. "It's not about me, ma'am," he told her. "It's Kaj. I don't think it's right to put him back out in a dangerous situation."

"Is he able to perform the tasks required of him by the mission?" she asked.

Cory could've lied and said no, Kaj wasn't up to it, but the lie would be obvious. Cory wasn't the only person who wrote reports about the dolphins. Commander Jackson already knew the answer to the question she had asked. Kaj was the best. She was trying to make a point.

"He is, ma'am, but —"

"That's all there is to it, then," she told him. Her face was set, emotionless. Any sympathy she had for Cory or for Kaj was buried deep below her official duties and her commitment to her mission. "You're a leader now, Chief McNab. It's not just your dolphin you're responsible for. Your team — the team you trained — *they* need you. You are the only dolphin handler with the experience to lead a covert marine mammal operation at this level of complexity and every one of them knows it. If you aren't there, it's not just the mission that suffers. Your *people* suffer. Remember that, Chief. We are trying to protect people, and the mammals in our care are tools to that end. They are not the end in themselves."

"So send me," he said. "Send me to lead without Kaj."

"We do not know how many operational dolphins the Russians have, nor how many mines they've littered their naval port with," she explained. "We need every qualified dolphin team we have on this operation, and I am not going to let one of our most valuable assets go unused because of sentimentality."

"Sentimentality?"

"Kaj is a dolphin," Commander Jackson snapped. "Don't forget that. He doesn't know the promises you made. He does what we've trained him to do. Any guilt or regret in this situation is coming entirely from you, and I suggest you stow it . . . right now. Your team needs you and the clock is ticking."

"Yes, ma'am," said Cory, his jaw clenched.

His commander took a deep breath and looked for a moment as if she were about to say something else, something softer, kinder — but she left him without another word, and he stood on the pier in dripping boots, his dolphin looking up at him from the water.

All around him the pier was a flurry of urgent activity, but Cory felt his feet rooted in place.

Of course Kaj didn't know Cory had made him a promise. So why did Cory feel so guilty? Was guilt purely a human feeling?

"One thousand two hundred and sixty pounds of fish ordered, Chief," Skunk interrupted his thoughts.

"What?" Cory startled.

"I requisitioned 1,260 pounds of mackerel to fly with us to Romania." Skunk looked proud of himself. "That's enough to feed five six-hundred-pound dolphins for seven days, assuming each dolphin eats six percent of his body weight daily. We'll have to resupply if we go longer than seven days." Skunk paused. "You think we will? Go longer, I mean?"

Cory shrugged but put his hand on the nervous young sailor's back. "If we do our jobs, we'll all be home in no time, safe and sound," he said.

He sure hoped he was right. Missions like this one had a way of being unpredictable. He worried he had just made another promise that he had no idea how to keep.

05:
GET WET

THE US Dock Landing Ship *McNamara* cut the waves at twenty knots, speeding from the port of Constanta on the Black Sea toward Sevastopol, over two hundred miles away. In a large cargo bay within the ship, the MK 6D team had set up five rigid inflatable tanks, one for each of their dolphins, strung with high netting so that the animals wouldn't fall out if the water got rough. Their equipment was stowed along the walls, out of the way. A portable walk-in freezer had been installed to hold a thousand-plus pounds of mackerel, and a large refrigerator held a variety of medical supplies. A mobile veterinary clinic had also been set up in the rear of the cargo hold, where the team's veterinarian, Dr. Morris, could perform exams, give shots, and even do emergency surgery on a dolphin if she needed to.

Hopefully, she wouldn't need to.

The dolphins were still stressed from the long flight, the truck ride, and being hauled onto the boat. It had been only two and a half days since they'd received their orders, and the team had done a great job deploying ahead of schedule. Cory was satisfied with everyone's performance, glad they had all taken their duties so seriously, and felt they were ready for the next phase of their mission.

In six hours, the transport phase would be over and Operation Open Water would begin.

In six hours, their dolphins would try to locate their first undersea explosives to clear a path for two Ukrainian warships stuck in the Russian-occupied port.

In six hours, they would find out just what exactly their enemy's dolphins were capable of.

Cory had to start thinking strategically, like a chess master, except the pieces he was moving were not plastic pawns and knights, but bomb-detecting dolphins and bomb-disposing humans. He had to hope his team could find mines faster than the other dolphins could stop them. If they failed and a Russian undersea mine sank a Ukrainian warship, or the Russians took control of the ships for themselves, the crisis could become a war.

Nobody wanted that to happen.

If they did everything right, it wouldn't happen. No one would get hurt. That was Cory's goal: to make sure they accomplished their mission without anyone having to draw a weapon.

The ship sailed for hours while the dolphins slept and the humans tried to. When they were a few miles from the harbor and the Russian naval base, their engines slowed, the *McNamara* turned to hold its position, and the executive officer announced their arrival.

"We're not going any closer," the lieutenant junior grade who had been present for the briefing back in San Diego told Cory. His name was Lieutenant Majeueski, which no one could manage to pronounce correctly. Cory just called him *Lieutenant* and did his best to avoid having to say his full name out loud. If the lieutenant noticed, he didn't say anything. He was probably used to it. "As far as we're telling the Russians, this is a training exercise and we're keeping our distance. We have small boats ready to deploy your team, the bomb disposal units, and my SEALs. How fast can your fish be in the water?"

"Dolphins are not fish, sir," Cory corrected him. He always felt the need to clarify this point. "They're aquatic mammals."

"They're military assets," the lieutenant corrected him grumpily. "How long before they can be in the water?"

"If we double-time, we can be moving in about an hour, sir."

"Very good, Chief," said the lieutenant. "I'll be in your boat, but operational control of the mission will be yours. Locate all undersea explosive ordnance and, once your dolphins are clear of the water, our bomb disposal unit will disarm them. When they give us the all-clear, we'll signal the Ukrainian ships that they can get out of port, and this will all be over before sunup.

"Sir, do we have any intelligence if the rebel forces in control of the port will let them leave?" Cory asked. Mines weren't the only concern. If missiles started firing from shore, he and his dolphins would be defenseless in their small rubber boats.

Cory could hardly believe he was asking such a question. He'd never thought he would have to think of so many "what ifs," but that was the nature of leadership. Like his father used to tell him, *Better to be prepared than to need repairs.*

"Chief, I'll be honest with you." The lieutenant sighed. "We have no idea what the rebels will do. This entire situation caught us by surprise."

"So, we also still don't know if they have dolphins of their own?"

"Correct," said the lieutenant. "We're going in blind."

"No, sir." Cory smiled. "Not blind. I think you'll be amazed by how much my dolphins can see."

"I like the confidence, McNab," the lieutenant told him. "Let's roll."

Cory saluted and went to the cargo hold to get their mission under way. They would have to load the dolphins from their individual pools onto portable rubber pads that sat on the back of high speed rigid-hull inflatable boats. Each boat would have a driver, a dolphin, the dolphin's handler, and two armed members of SEAL Team Five. In addition to the five dolphin RHIBs, there would be three other boats with equipment to disarm the mines once the dolphins found them, and there would be two boats that had only Navy SEALs on them, armed with heavy machine guns in case they ran into trouble. All in all, there would be over fifty sailors taking part in this complicated mission, and though several of them held ranks higher than Cory's, he was the specialist in the use and care of military dolphins, and he was to be in command.

"Well, Kaj," he told his dolphin. "You ready to saddle up one more time?"

Kaj slapped the water, splashing Cory's blue camo utilities from shoulder to shoes. He thought it was playtime again. Kaj always thought it was playtime. Cory looked around to make sure his team wasn't watching him. He didn't want Preeti to see him fooling around, and he didn't want Skunk to think it was okay to goof off.

They were all busy with their own dolphins, so Cory reached through the netting and splashed water back at Kaj. Kaj clicked blissfully and Cory stared into his eyes, searching for a sign that the dolphin understood what was being asked of him.

Of course he didn't. He was a dolphin.

They didn't understand the reasons for their missions. Then again, Cory didn't much understand the reasons, either. He, like his dolphin, did what he was told to do and tried to do it well.

He left Kaj's pool and found Dr. Morris going over her checklists.

"Everything set?" he asked her. "You have everything you need?"

"My people will be standing by," she said. "We'll have a surgical harness ready in case of emergencies and we've got a cargo helicopter on the mainland on notice in case we need one of your mammals air-lifted out."

"Roger that," said Cory.

"Just try to make sure we don't need any of that," the veterinarian added. "I'd much rather be bored on this deployment, giving vitamin shots, not removing bullets from fins."

"If they want to shoot one of my dolphins, they'll have to go through me first," said Cory, hoping his confidence sounded convincing. What he wanted so much to tell her was that he was terrified for the safety of his dolphin, terrified of failure, and terrified that in a moment of high danger, he would not know what to do when the rest of his team looked to him, and his hesitation would get them killed.

But he didn't say a word. The problem with being a leader, he found, was that he had no one to talk to about his fears.

Suddenly, a bell sounded and the large docking bay door began to open, letting the cool night air fill the cargo hold, the sea-salt smell mixing with the heavy scents of fish and sweat and bleach.

"All right, Mark Sixty, let's get wet!" he shouted.

They worked together, attaching each dolphin's harness to a crane. One by one they lifted the animals into the air and drove them to the end of the cargo bay, where their rigid-hull inflatable boats waited in the water.

The dolphins were placed on board, tails bent up toward the sky, heads lifted in eager anticipation. With every step of the way, each dolphin's handler stayed in front of them, giving them fish, patting them, and saying comforting words. Preeti went first with Kojak, followed by Cruz and his dolphin, Zeus. Tully and Keanu followed them, and Cory and Skunk watched each boat hit the water and peel off. The dolphins were perched on the stern of the boats, their pads hung slightly over the side so that they could jump on and off easily. The driver stood in the middle behind the wheel, and the Special Forces Operators, as they were called, knelt, two per boat, beside a heavy machine gun at the front. The dolphin handlers sat next to their dolphins.

"Breathe," Cory told Skunk. "You've trained for this. You're ready."

"Chief," Skunk replied. "I know you don't think I'm ready. I know you didn't want me here."

"I didn't want me here, either, Skunk," Cory said. "But we're here now and we've got a job to do. Don't worry about what I think. Worry about you and your dolphin finding and marking those undersea mines."

"Roger that," said Skunk.

"You're up," Cory told him, and they loaded Tomas into his boat. Skunk hopped aboard after, and Cory was left in the cargo hold with Kaj. The loading crew had the harness ready. Cory stepped up to the edge of the pool and put out his hand. Kaj opened his mouth, revealing a row of razor-sharp teeth. Cory stuck his hand into Kaj's mouth and scratched the dolphin's tongue, just how he liked. Kaj's tail bent upward, the flukes on the end shimmering in the fluorescent light of the cargo hold.

"We got this, pal," he told Kaj, then motioned for the crane to hoist.

Ten minutes later, Cory was sitting beside Kaj, cruising at the front of a small fleet of black rubber boats, nearly invisible on the surface of the water as they motored toward the flashing lights of the warships in port. Through his earpiece he heard his boat pilots talking to one another, maintaining formation.

When they were about a mile away from the big warships, Cory signaled for his small fleet to stop. He clicked on his radio and spoke to his dolphin team.

"This is Mark One Actual." From here on out, he would use their mission call sign for the dolphin teams. *Actual* told everyone over the radio that it was the team leader himself speaking, not just someone on his boat. "Mark Two, get wet."

He listened for the splash as Preeti's dolphin slipped from the pad into the water to begin the hunt for mines. The dolphins had never been in the Black Sea before, but they would easily be able to orient themselves with their bio-sonar and find their way around. It was a remarkable thing about dolphins, how well they navigated wherever they were. If a dolphin got lost, you could be sure something was wrong. Dolphins did not normally get lost — not in the wild, and certainly not in the navy.

Even if their dolphins did somehow get lost, each had a small radio ID tag installed under their skin. It was the same technology dog owners use to microchip their beloved pets. You couldn't exactly slip a collar onto a dolphin with a tag that said "If found, please return to the United States Navy," so the radio ID tags were the next best thing. The little chip didn't send a strong enough signal to track the dolphins over long distances, but it could be used to identify them if they swam off and were later found elsewhere. Of course, the navy had never actually lost a dolphin before, but the ID tags gave everyone peace of mind.

"Mark Two is in the water," Preeti said over the radio.

"Mark Three, Mark Four, go," Cory ordered.

He heard the splash and confirmation of two more dolphins in the water.

"Mark Five, go."

There was a pause. He heard a dolphin's clicking carried on the night air, probably Skunk needing a bit more communication to get Tomas doing what he wanted, but a second later, the splash came and Tomas was in the water, too.

"Mark One is a go," he said, then he turned to Kaj.

The dolphin's eyes gazed at him, shining. Cory bent his arm so that it looked like he was making a chicken wing, and Kaj raised his right flipper. Cory took out a heavy rubber strap with a deepwater camera on it and slipped it onto Kaj's flipper so that it sat just at the point where the fin met his body. Then he held up one fist, opened his palm, and swept his arm sideways. Following the motion, Kaj heaved his belly and slid off the pad, entering the water with hardly any noise at all. An instant later, his head popped up beside the boat, awaiting further instructions.

The dolphins were all trained to respond to visual cues and gestures so that the handlers didn't have to speak or blow whistles on a covert mission. They could operate in almost total silence if they had to. Cory made another gesture, his index finger extended and his hand circling, a motion like telling a helicopter to take off.

Kaj raised himself up out of the water a little higher and then, with one powerful flick of his tail, vanished below the surface.

Cory looked at the video feed on his tablet. He could swipe between the views from the cameras on each of the five dolphins, but otherwise all he could do was watch, and wait, and hope.

The hunt for undersea explosives had begun.

06:
SWIMMER NULLIFICATION

THERE were five dolphins in the water, all searching for hidden explosives.

Sea mines were designed to explode when hit by large objects, like ships, but not to explode when bumped by sea life swimming past, like dolphins. That was one of the reasons dolphins were so effective in the hunt for dangerous submerged explosives.

They could also swim deeper and faster than any human could ever go. What might take a human scuba diver several hours to find, a dolphin could find in a matter of minutes. Even watching through the cameras, Cory couldn't really see what the dolphins saw.

For him, the night-vision lens showed the undersea world in a ghostly green haze, with flashes of light glinting off the eyes of fish as they darted away from the racing dolphins. He caught the occasional glimpse of another of their dolphins swimming ahead of a camera, but mostly, he saw the dark of open water. Even when the dolphin rose to the surface to breathe, he couldn't make much out. The moon was shrouded in clouds and none of their boats had running lights on.

The dolphins, however, could see everything.

Aside from having excellent eyesight, even in the dark, dolphins have a unique bio-sonar that uses echolocation, sending out waves of sound that bounce back to them through the water and show them objects that might otherwise be invisible. In the wild, this bio-sonar helps them find fish to eat. In the service of the military, they'd been trained to use it for bomb-finding.

People still don't fully understand how it works. A dolphin's jaws, bent into that permanent dolphin grin, are uniquely suited to carrying vibrating sound waves up to their head, and the big, round bump on the dolphin's head in front of their blowhole — called the *melon* — also plays some role in allowing the dolphin to "see" with these sound waves. What, exactly, the dolphin sees, is a mystery — but time and time again, on mission after mission, the dolphins in the navy's care had proven that it works. They could tell the difference between different kinds of undersea mines that looked identical to the human eye.

If one of Cory's dolphins found a mine, it would swim back to its handler's boat — which they also knew how to find, no matter how far away they'd swum — and it would tap a tennis ball hanging off the side with its snout. Then the handler would attach a small beacon to the dolphin's snout, and it would return straightaway to what it had found and, using a suction cup on the end of the beacon, stick it to the mine.

After that, the explosives disposal unit would follow the beacon, dive underwater, and disarm the mine. That part of the job didn't involve Cory's team. Their goal was just to mark the mines. If they could find a path out of the port without needing to take the time to disarm all of them, that's what the navy would want to do. None of that could start, however, until the dolphins started finding something.

And that was taking a while.

Fifteen minutes had passed and though the dolphins kept popping up to the surface to breathe, none of them was returning to their handlers with a sign.

"Maybe there aren't any mines in the port after all," suggested Cory's boat pilot. "Maybe they sent us all the way out here for nothing."

"Or maybe they're using a new kind of mine your fish can't see," the lieutenant suggested.

Cory started to correct the young officer again, then just fell back into silence. He didn't feel like giving a biology lesson to a guy he was supposed to call *sir*, especially when the guy was carrying enough weaponry to invade a small country by himself. Navy SEALs were a different breed than just about anyone else in the navy, and Cory figured the guy could do his job just as well, whether or not he remembered that dolphins were actually mammals. Like people, they breathe air, are warm-blooded, give birth to live young (as opposed to laying eggs, like most fish), have some kind of body hair, and feed milk to their young. Unlike people, they live in the ocean and have fins. Still, that didn't make them fish, any more than having sneakers made Cory a professional athlete.

He checked his watch and waited. He had faith in his dolphins.

"Ten bucks says Tomas makes a find first," Skunk whispered over the radio.

"Make it twenty," Preeti responded. "You don't stand a shot."

"Cut out the comm chatter," Cory barked at them. "Anyway, Kaj'll be back first, so neither of you would win that bet."

One of the good things about being the team leader was that the rest of his team couldn't talk back to him. It was easy to win every argument when you were the boss.

It also helped that he was right.

A moment later, in a flash of glistening silver, Kaj popped from the water with a blast of air from his blowhole. He tapped the tennis ball hanging from the side of Cory's boat with his snout. He'd found something.

Cory sprang into action, tossing a chunk of fish into Kaj's mouth, then attaching the beacon to his snout. He patted Kaj on the head and gave him the hand signal to go mark the undersea mine.

"Found a peanut," Cory announced over the radio, which was their code for a mine. "Disposal team, stand by."

"Roger that," confirmed the explosives disposal team.

"Peanut," Preeti announced, indicating that her dolphin had also found a mine.

"Got one here, too," Skunk said, just seconds after Preeti's announcement. Even over the radio, he sounded annoyed that she'd beaten him. Still, Cory was impressed. He hadn't expected Skunk and Tomas to find anything at all.

Over the next fifteen minutes, the dolphin teams identified and marked twelve undersea mines that had been planted to block the escape of the ships. On the screen, Cory watched each dolphin dive to the devices, which he saw were floating anywhere from twenty to fifty feet below the surface of the water, tethered to the seafloor by large chains. Each time, the dolphin would tap the explosive with the device on his nose, which attached the plunger beacon, then swim away. It happened so fast, the screen mostly showed the action as a choppy blur. Not even their camera technology was advanced enough to keep up with their dolphins.

After four trips to four different undersea mines, Kaj came back and signaled to Cory that there weren't any more to find. The other dolphins signaled the same to their handlers.

"We've found all the peanuts," Cory announced over the radio. "Let's get them out of their shells."

That was the code to begin disarming them.

"Roger that," the bomb disposal technician answered. "Divers in the water."

"Okay, Mark Sixty," Cory called his team. "Bring your partners back on board."

Cory waved his arm and Kaj jumped back onto the pad in a perfect slide. He bent his tail up and clicked happily with his blowhole, opening his mouth for a reward. Cory tossed him a fish.

"Nicely done," he said. He felt good.

They'd done their part of the mission without any problems and they'd done it in under an hour. Now it would be a few hours of work for the divers to disarm all the mines they'd found, but come sunup, there would be a clear path out of the harbor and the two ships trapped in port would be gone.

"Oh, come on!" Skunk grunted, apparently unaware that his radio link was still active. "Get up here!"

"Mark Five, this is Mark One Actual," Cory said. "What's your situation?"

"Tomas doesn't want to get out of the water," he said. "I think he was having too much fun."

"Mark Five, get him out now!" Cory ordered.

"I'm trying, boss!"

A full minute later, Skunk confirmed that his dolphin was back on board the boat. Cory rolled his eyes and the lieutenant on board shrugged. Cory's issues with his team were not the lieutenant's problem.

They waited silently in their boats while the bomb disposal teams worked. Every few minutes Cory would pour a pitcher of seawater over Kaj. He patted his partner on the head, rubbed his flippers, and kept himself busy keeping Kaj comfortable.

Until the radio crackled to life.

"Mark One Actual, this is EOD One Actual." The voice over the radio belonged to the leader of the Explosive Ordnance Disposal unit — the bomb defusers. His voice was garbled because he was speaking through a microphone in his dive mask. Cory knew that meant he was underwater, working on one of the undersea mines.

"Mark One Actual," Cory confirmed he was on the radio.

"Are all your systems clear of the area?" the diver

asked. He wanted to know if all the dolphins were out of the water.

"Affirmative," Cory said. He paused, thinking. "Mark Five, confirm?"

"Tomas is with me," Skunk confirmed.

"We're all clear," Cory repeated for the bomb technician.

"We've got some activity around us," the technician reported. "Looks like one dolphin. He's circling my area. Looks like he's — AHH!"

There was a screech over the radio, a sound like an underwater scream.

"Mark One Actual, this is Disposal Two!" another technician came on the radio, breathless. "Our chief's been hit. A dolphin came out of nowhere and . . . he . . . rammed him in the chest. Hit him with some kind of a . . . some kind of needle thing. He's pushed him up to the surface . . . I think he's coming back down to —"

Suddenly, there was another roar of bubbles over the radio.

"Disposal Two?" Cory called out. "Disposal Two, report!"

He didn't get a reply.

"Disposal Three," another voice crackled. "We need a medic. The chief's unconscious. He's not breathing! I think he's —"

"This is Disposal Two," another voice said. "I'm on the surface. I think that dolphin broke my ribs. He hit me so fast, then was gone. I don't know where he went . . . Wait, I think I see —"

The voice cut off again.

"Disposal Two, report!" Cory demanded. "Disposal Three, do you copy?"

There was no answer.

Cory's blood turned to ice in his veins. He remembered the words from the briefing: *swimmer nullification*.

He pictured the "kill dart" they'd seen in the lieutenant commander's presentation, the needle on the end of a tank; the rumored training of the Russian dolphins to be lethal weapons.

"This is Mark One Actual," Cory barked quickly into the radio. "All divers out of the water, ASAP. Get your guys out now!"

Cory knew precisely what was happening. There was an enemy dolphin in the water, armed and trained to kill. And it was going to pick off the navy's divers one by one.

07:
PICKING A FIGHT

IN the water, a human being is no match for a dolphin. A dolphin can see perfectly, no matter how dark the night or how black the sea. They hunt by sound as well as sight; they move with the speed of a torpedo, and their strength is unmatched by any other denizen of the deep. In the water, they are at the top of the food chain. There are no natural predators who hunt them. Even sharks are afraid of dolphins.

The dolphin in the water with the navy divers hadn't been trained to hunt for sharks, though. It had been trained to hunt people. There was no way the divers could get out in time, not without help. The dolphin had them at its mercy.

The lieutenant from SEAL Team Five ordered three of his boats to move in. "I'm sending my divers in to get those men out of the water," he told Cory.

"Sir, I must advise against that," Cory said. "We don't know how many dolphins we're up against, and your guys will just be additional targets for them."

"My guys can handle themselves," the lieutenant responded.

"Respectfully, sir," Cory replied, "not even your best man can avoid these animals, outswim them, or outsmart them. Their echolocation allows them to see right through skin and locate a person's vital organs. That means they can target a human's heart, lungs, whatever . . . and slam into that spot with more force than a truck going full speed on a highway. One blow can be fatal, and that's from a dolphin who isn't wearing a kill dart on its snout."

"Then at least the dolphin will be targeting my guys instead of the minesweepers we've been sent to protect," the lieutenant said. "Our job is to draw fire. Whether it's coming from humans or giant fish, it doesn't make one difference to me. We're here for security and we're going to provide it."

He picked up the radio, about to order his men into the water, knowing the risk and willing to risk it anyway. That kind of danger was what the Navy SEALs signed up for when they joined the toughest Special Forces unit in the world.

But they weren't in charge of this op. Cory was.

He stopped the lieutenant, placing his own hand on the radio. Whether they were willing or not, he couldn't let these men put themselves in mortal danger when he could prevent it.

He looked at Kaj, saw the eager glint of the dolphin's eyes as he awaited another gesture of instruction. Every dolphin in the program was trained to protect a port from swimmer attacks, and it seemed the Russian dolphin was trained the same way.

The only way to stop it would be with his own dolphins.

He got on the radio. "This is Mark One Actual," he announced. "All Mark Sixty teams, prepare to deploy your system."

He realized after he said it that he'd used the word *system* instead of *dolphin*. It was a mental trick to distance himself from what he was asking them to do.

"What instruction do we give?" Preeti's voice came back.

Cory had never imagined that his dolphins would need to protect swimmers from other dolphins in enemy territory. How would he even give that order? What possible series of gestures could communicate what he wanted them to do?

Training a dolphin was a slow process of rewarding tiny, individual tasks one by one, until they could be combined into more complicated behaviors. In the dolphin program, a new animal was trained first to recognize its handler, then to come to its handler when signaled, then to roll, to jump, to open its mouth, to find a toy, to decide between several toys, and so on, learning to recognize its handler's basic instructions, then to do them in order. Desired behaviors were taught and rewarded, while unwanted behaviors were ignored until the dolphin could do all kinds of things they would never do in the wild, like sit still for a tooth cleaning, jump through a series of hoops, or identify certain kinds undersea explosive mines. One thing they couldn't be taught how to do was tell a friend from an enemy. If they were ordered to hit swimmers, they would hit any and all swimmers, whoever they were.

Except, as far as Cory knew, no dolphin had ever been trained to *protect* a swimmer. He knew they did it sometimes, even in the wild, but it wasn't learned behavior. It wasn't something he could order his dolphins to do.

He wracked his brain, searching for some instruction he could give that would protect the divers from the enemy dolphin.

In the wild, he knew, dolphins were territorial. They had their hunting areas and their pods, and every pod had its own way of doing things. Some pods used tools like seashells for digging on the ocean floor and some didn't. Some pods helped their weaker members capture fish and some abandoned their weaker members. Sometimes they didn't get along with other pods. Sometimes they fought each other.

Cory had to call on that natural instinct and hope the dolphins in the United States Navy wouldn't like a dolphin that they didn't know.

Basically, he had to send his dolphins into the water to pick a fight.

"Tell them it's time to play capture the ball," he said, which was a game they used in training to socialize the dolphins with each other. It was exactly what it sounded like. One ball, five dolphins, and they were each rewarded for getting the ball and throwing it to one of the other dolphins in a certain order until they'd all gotten to swim with it. It was a way of teaching them to cooperate with the rest of their team.

Cory hoped the Russian dolphin would want to play, too.

His dolphins were not trained to let anyone else join their game.

He pulled out the big red ball from one of the storage bins on board. He held it up, and Kaj's eyes tracked it eagerly. Cory had to remind himself that the smile on his dolphin's face was not a sign of friendliness. He hoped his dolphin knew how to be a bit of a bully.

He threw the ball into the water, then gestured for Kaj to begin the game.

With a loud splash, Kaj flung himself off his pad, dove below the water, and burst up to grab the ball from underneath. He jumped so high that even the flukes of his tail cleared the water by over two feet.

He was, briefly, the perfect shadow of a dolphin against the night sky.

Then he plummeted again into the water and raced to find the other dolphins in his navy pod, clutching the ball tightly in his jaws.

"Deploy!" Cory called into the radio, then cringed as he heard the sound of another diver hit by dolphin. He also heard a thumping sound in the air. It grew louder and louder. A helicopter. For a moment, he feared they were about to be attacked from the air as well as under the sea, but the helicopter wasn't coming from shore. It was coming from the direction of their ship.

"Medevac choppers inbound!" the lieutenant said. They'd been called to evacuate the injured divers to the *McNamara*'s sick bay. He hadn't even thought to call them, it had all happened so fast. Luckily, someone else had. On board the other small boats in the covert fleet, he knew that navy corpsmen — the medics — were working frantically to save the wounded divers. He didn't think all of them would survive their wounds. A dolphin was an expert killer.

But still, he should have remembered to call for the medevac himself. Could those lost moments have cost another sailor his life?

He pushed away the dark thoughts and looked at the screen on his tablet. He could see the big ball gripped in Kaj's mouth as the dolphin darted just below the surface. Suddenly, another dolphin was visible beside him, a sleek streak of gray flesh and rippling muscle.

Kaj jumped from the water and, in midair, released the ball. The other dolphin, Preeti's partner, Kojak, caught it in his jaws and entered the water again with a splash. Cory switched to the view from Kojak's camera. He saw a flash of gray below, another dolphin circling, then coming straight up for Kojak, mouth open with rows of shining white teeth. Just before impact, the dolphin turned and Cory recognized Tomas. The two dolphins surfaced together, repeated the ball toss, and Tomas dove with it in his jaws, a perfect maneuver.

"Come on," Cory whispered to himself. "Come on, you lousy caviar-eating sea monster! Where are you?"

The SEAL lieutenant shook his head in disbelief. He looked ready to call in SEALs any second if something useful didn't happen soon.

Just then, there was another flash of gray in the deep. As it rose toward Tomas, Cory's heart raced. It wasn't a dolphin he recognized. He saw that it had a device attached to the end of its snout: a kind of small air tank, just like the tank they'd seen in the briefing, the system that injected carbon dioxide into a swimmer when the dolphin rammed him.

The "killer dolphin" had come out to play.

When the dolphin reached Tomas, it didn't turn. Its mouth opened and it tried to bite the ball out of Tomas's grip. Tomas dodged and the two dolphins slammed into each other sideways.

Cory switched views and saw Cruz's dolphin, Zeus, swimming straight for the unfamiliar dolphin, and then he switched to Kaj's view, racing up to join the fracas. Kaj had aimed straight at the enemy dolphin's rib cage, but the dolphin twirled and dove at the last instant, dodging the hit.

"Looks like you got your fish fight," the lieutenant said.

"Sir, just make sure they get the rest of the divers out of the water fast," Cory told him, then went back to the screen.

Though he'd stopped the attack on the divers, he

didn't feel good about it. Tricking dolphins into fighting each other was wrong, and he knew it. Animals might not know what war was, or whose side they fought for or why, but one thing they did know was the oldest law of nature:

Kill or be killed.

08:
THE LAW OF THE SEA

THIS was going to be an ugly fight, and it was five dolphins against one, but that one had a weapon on the end of its nose. It was like something out of a bad sci-fi movie. *Attack Dolphins of the Deep!*

Except this was real, and Cory felt responsible for it. But what choice did he have? People were hurt, maybe dying. He had to get that dolphin away from the divers somehow.

The other dolphin had surfaced to breathe, then twisted around to go after Zeus, who'd gotten the ball from Tomas.

Kaj reached the dolphin before it hit Zeus. His jaws opened wide and then shut fast as he approached, making a loud snap that warned the other dolphin to back off.

The dolphin spun toward Kaj. Kaj dove below it, flipped over, and propelled himself quickly upward with a mighty thrust of his tail. The other dolphin tried to turn around on him, but Kaj was too fast and his jaws closed on the dolphin's tail. Through the screen on his tablet, Cory saw the water cloud with a green mist.

The mist was only green because of the night-vision filter. If he'd actually been in the water, he knew, the mist would have been red.

Kaj had drawn first blood.

Tomas charged forward and slammed his hard snout into the bleeding dolphin's side. The dolphin spun, bubbles erupting from its blowhole as it swam up to take a breath. Kaj mercilessly rushed after it, blocking the dolphin from surfacing for air, knocking it down by hitting it with his full length.

Cory watched from Kaj's view as Tomas and the other dolphin locked in a fight. They swam around each other in corkscrews, twirling and biting, trying to keep each other from coming up for air, trying to sink their jaws into each other's faces.

Tomas had a toothy bite mark along his left flank. The other dolphin was moving faster. It flipped itself over and managed to get Tomas's fin in its jaws, was about to rip out a chunk when Kojak hit from underneath, breaking the grip, and then Kaj bolted forward, snapping his jaws again to frighten the enemy away.

This time, it seemed to work. The dolphin dove to escape, but Tomas, not ready to give up, swam under it to block its path.

The enemy dolphin would not be stopped. It rammed Tomas forcefully out of the way, jabbing a deep puncture wound into Tomas's head, just below his blowhole. Tomas, unfazed, tried to bite it as it passed, but in a few quick flips of its tail, the other dolphin disappeared down into the dark sea. Tomas swam after it a moment, then let it go when he saw

Keanu swimming up to the rest of the pod, the big red ball gripped firmly in his mouth.

For the dolphins, this had all been a violent game of keep-away, and, it seemed, they'd won.

The water was cloudy with blood and Cory worried it might summon sharks to the area. Five dolphins could easily take on a single shark, but five injured dolphins in the middle of a feeding frenzy would be in trouble.

"Call back your systems," Cory ordered. "We're clear."

The handlers signaled their dolphins back. Cory watched on screen as Keanu breached the surface, jumping half out of the water and falling back in on his side, making as big a splash as possible. He repeated the victory jump three more times, before Kaj approached and jumped with him, snatching the ball in midair as they leapt. Keanu let him take it, and the moment Kaj hit the water, all five dolphins turned in different directions and swam for their handlers' boats.

"All swimmers clear of the water," a diver from the bomb disposal team announced over the radio. Up above, the helicopters drew closer, preparing to lower down stretchers to evacuate the wounded.

Kaj popped up beside Cory's boat with the big red ball in his mouth. Cory signaled for him to jump onto his pad, and once on, Kaj dropped the ball and opened his mouth for a fish. There were smears of blood and bits of dolphin blubber wedged between his teeth.

Cory tossed him a fish, just as the order came for all units to abort mission and return to the ship.

"Mark Sixty, this is Mark One Actual," Cory said into the radio, as their boats turned to motor at full speed for home. The helicopters overhead peeled away. "I need a sitrep."

"Mark Two," Preeti said. "We'll need the vet. We've got some injuries. Mostly scrapes. They look minor."

"Mark Three, same," Cruz said.

"Mark Four," said Tully. "Keanu's doing fine."

"Mark Five," Skunk reported in. "Uh . . . some blood," he said. "A lot of scrapes. I think Tomas might have lost some teeth, too. He's bleeding a lot, actually."

"Roger that," said Cory. "Vet is on standby. ETA to *McNamara* is twenty-five minutes. Administer first aid."

"I . . ." Skunk sounded hesitant.

"Stop the bleeding," Cory instructed. "Just like you would on a human. Apply pressure to the wound."

All the handlers were trained in the basics of dolphin care. They knew how to stop bleeding, stitch a wound, even how to brush a dolphin's teeth.

"I think I got it," said Skunk. "He's calming down. The bleeding's slowing."

"Good," said Cory. He closed his eyes and gave silent thanks to the universe. He couldn't tell if he wanted to cheer or weep.

Skunk could hold it together until Dr. Morris could take care of Tomas. Cory already imagined the scolding he would get from the veterinarian for deliberately putting the dolphins in harm's way, but he'd made a split-second decision to save human lives, and thankfully, none of his dolphins had died in the process.

The mission, however, was a failure.

They had marked, but not cleared, the undersea explosives. Unfortunately, the warships trapped in port were too big to avoid them. There was no clear path out. The mines would still have to be disarmed, but the navy couldn't send divers into the water again while that dolphin was still a threat. It might take months to train the navy dolphins to protect the bomb disposal teams from an enemy dolphin, if it were even possible to train them to do that. How could you teach a dolphin to have an enemy?

And, now that he'd tricked them into fighting once, Cory had doubts that setting dolphin against dolphin was even the least bit ethical. There was nothing moral or good about a person making animals fight each other, no matter the reason.

He knew for a fact that it was also illegal.

The navy had to follow the rules set forth in the Marine Mammal Protection Act and the Animal

Welfare Act, both federal laws passed by Congress and signed by the president that told people and research facilities what they could, should, and could not do to the animals in their care.

Sending five of them to harass and attack a killer dolphin in a foreign sea was most certainly a violation of both those laws.

In his desperation to save lives, Cory, it seemed, had become a criminal.

09:
TAKING CASUALTIES

CORY rested his hand on Kaj's back as their boat raced home to the *McNamara*. He patted his partner, just in front of his blowhole, then he rubbed the dolphin's pectoral fins, just how Kaj liked. He even scratched his tongue a bit, before he went back to rubbing him down and dumping cool seawater over his body.

As he ran his hands over the smooth dolphin skin, he felt rough patches, scratches and abrasions. He wiped away some blood, but the dolphin didn't appear to be bleeding. Kaj would need to be cleaned and rubbed with ointment to prevent infection. He'd need to have his blood drawn and tested for contamination, for poison, for anything out of the ordinary that could cause him harm. It did appear, however, that'd he'd come out of the fight okay.

"I'm so sorry I put you through that, buddy," he told the dolphin. He touched the old scars from past missions. "But you did a great job. You always do a great job."

He didn't say out loud the thought that passed through his mind: *You shouldn't have to*.

"Quick thinking, Chief McNab," the SEAL lieutenant told him, shouting over the loud boat engine.

"Thank you, sir," Cory said back.

"You put your team at risk to protect my guys," the SEAL said. "I'm grateful."

Cory just nodded. He wasn't sure he had done the right thing, and with every minute that passed, his doubts grew, spreading like a cloud of blood in the water.

The Navy SEALs were Special Forces operatives who were trained for risking their lives. They knew the dangers they might face when they signed up to become Navy SEALs. They worked amazingly hard for the opportunity to face those risks, in fact. Eight out of every ten SEAL recruits dropped out of training in the first phase of it. Cory himself had dropped out of SEAL training years ago. The sailors who do make it, the ones who do join the SEAL teams, do so with pride and often eagerness to face danger. Some of them had even told Cory they enjoyed it. To an elite few, a day without danger was like a day without sunshine.

The dolphins, on the other hand, had no idea why they were doing what they were doing and they had no desire to seek out danger. They had not chosen to be in the navy or to serve their country. They *had* no country. They were bred and held in captivity. They were raised from dolphin calves to know only their sea cages, their handlers' signals, their rewards of fish and play. They did what they were told simply because they knew no other life. They were not wild and they were not free. What right did Cory have to order them to fight? What right did any human have over them?

And yet, Cory was a leader. He was responsible for the sailors on his mission, like Commander Jackson had said.

His choice to send in the dolphins meant some divers would be going home to their families who might not have been going home alive otherwise.

The responsibility made his head hurt.

Just when he thought he couldn't possibly feel worse, his radio crackled to life.

"Mark One Actual, this is Mark Five," Skunk's voice blared in his ear.

"Go ahead, Five," Cory answered.

"It's Tomas," Skunk said. "Something's gotten worse. He's . . . he's having some kind of seizure. It's shaking the whole boat like crazy."

"Roger that," said Cory, keeping his voice calm. "Can you keep him alive until we get to Dr. Morris?"

"I . . . I don't . . . uh . . ." Skunk was in a panic.

"Mark Five, listen up," Cory snapped. "Dolphins need their hearts beating and their lungs full of air to live, just like people. You've been trained for this. You've got emergency medical equipment on board. Use your training. Remember your training and keep him alive for a few more minutes. Can you do that?"

"Yes . . . uh, yes, Chief," Skunk said.

"Very good," Cory told him and clicked off. His voice had stayed firm, but his hand was shaking.

He pulled up the long-range satellite phone to call in to Dr. Morris. "We've got a Code Blue coming in," he said, which would scramble the veterinary team to get a dolphin out of the boat and into surgery the moment they reached the ship's cargo bay. A crane would be in position, a surgical harness and table prepared. Dr. Morris would be sterile and ready to operate. They could even get a helicopter to evacuate the dolphin if they needed to. The navy took care of its own when they got hurt in the line of duty, even when "its own" meant a six-hundred-pound bottlenose dolphin.

"All teams clear the way for Mark Five," Cory ordered. The docking door was open, so Skunk's boat sped right up the ramp, cutting the engines just before it went in. As they sped past and disappeared into the giant hull, Cory saw Skunk kneeling on the pad beside the seven-foot-long dolphin, his hands pressed against Tomas's wound, trying to stop the bleeding.

By the time Cory's boat was on board and he jumped out into six inches of water, Tomas was already being rushed to surgery. Dr. Morris's team surrounded the injured dolphin, who was strapped to a rolling table, and Skunk stood alone, shivering in his soaking wet suit, staring forward blankly.

The other dolphins were being loaded carefully into their pools, where the other handlers could check them out and administer minor first aid.

"His heart wasn't beating anymore," Skunk muttered. He looked up at Cory, tears in his eyes. "His heart had already stopped."

"Doc Morris has the best team there is," said Cory. "They'll do everything they can to bring him back. Dolphins are tougher than we can imagine. They're like Wolverine. You like Wolverine?" Cory tried to distract him.

Skunk just shook his head. "Spider-Man," he said.

Cory didn't know what to say about Spider-Man.

"Did all the divers survive?" Skunk asked.

Cory glanced back at the SEAL lieutenant, who was on a phone speaking to officers in the ship's command center. He looked at Cory and shook his head sadly, and held up two fingers.

Two dead. It could have been worse. There had been a dozen more in the water and they all got out. Some had probably been wounded pretty badly, but there could have been a lot more fatalities if the dolphins hadn't come to the rescue, if Tomas hadn't scared that Russian dolphin back to its handler. Tomas was a hero.

That wasn't much comfort for Skunk, though, or for Tomas, who couldn't know that he'd saved so many human lives. A dolphin couldn't know *why* he had been hurt, only that he was hurt. How did you comfort a dolphin? How did you tell him his sacrifice was worth it? How could a dolphin understand?

How could a person?

Skunk's knees quivered and Cory held him up.

"What's it for?" Skunk wondered. "What is all this for?"

Cory didn't know how to answer.

10:
PUNCHLINES

CORY'S team of handlers sat together in the mess, poking at sad lumps of scrambled eggs and greasy hash browns on plastic trays. It was breakfast time.

Breakfast? thought Cory. *I hadn't even noticed the sun come up.*

Tomas was still in surgery, and the other dolphins were all below in their pools, sleeping. Sort of.

Dolphins never fully sleep the way humans do. They are not involuntary breathers, which means every breath they take is a choice. They have to decide to surface, then decide to breathe, then dive again underwater. Even in sleep, half of their brain is active, telling them to swim, to surface, to breathe. No one knows exactly what goes on in a dolphin's mind when it's asleep, but there is a lot of brain activity. Cory wondered if dolphins dreamed, and if they did, could they have nightmares? Was he responsible for giving these dolphins nightmares? The thought was silly, but he couldn't shake it from his mind.

"Doc says Tomas has a collapsed lung and serious internal bleeding," Skunk told them. His voice came out scratchy with exhaustion. He looked about ten years older than he had just hours ago. His streak of white hair seemed whiter than before. Cory's mind was playing tricks on him. "Puncture wounds from the dart that Russian dolphin was wearing."

"Doc Morris is good," Cory assured him. "She'll do everything she can to save him."

Skunk jabbed a fork into his plate so hard that the tray bounced.

Cruz and Tully quietly moved their eggs around their plates. Preeti ate quickly, with the practice of a soldier who had been trained to eat at chow time, no matter how sick she felt.

"Tomas saved the lives of a lot of divers out there," Preeti told Skunk. "He did his job well. No point crying about it."

Skunk looked up at her with bloodshot eyes. "Sorry for *feeling*. We can't all be as hard core as you, SB-1 Suraj. Some of us actually *chose* to work with dolphins because we care about them."

"I care about them," she said. "That's why I respect the sacrifice Tomas made out there today."

"Admit it," said Skunk. "You don't even want to be here. You were *transferred* in. You'd rather be with them."

He nodded toward a table where some of the men from SEAL Team Five were eating breakfast with the Special Warfare Combatant-Craft Crewmen, the team that Preeti had been training to join before the navy reassigned her to the dolphin program. They all shoveled the food into their mouths like they'd be called away from the table at any second, and they didn't pay any attention to anyone else in the room. The Special Forces teams were a world unto themselves. Cory could see in Preeti's eyes: the longing to join them. Skunk obviously saw it, too, and he took all his fear and his hurt and he threw them in Preeti's face.

"They didn't want you," he told her coldly.

Preeti looked like she wanted to jump across the table and impale him with a fork.

Cruz and Tully looked between the other two dolphin handlers, tense, waiting to see who would strike first. It wouldn't be a fair fight, just like it hadn't been with the dolphins. Skunk didn't stand a chance if Preeti's fist flew.

Cory had to stop his team from falling apart in front of him. He had to stop his team from fighting each other.

They still had to serve together, and for all he knew they would be ordered out on the water again when the sun went down. The mission was far from over and they needed to cooperate, not fight.

To break the tension, he said the first thing that came into his mind: "What do you call a dolphin with no eyes?"

The rest of Cory's team looked at him like he was crazy.

"Dol*phn*," he told them.

Cruz let out a small groan. Cory kept going.

"What did the dolphin say when he spilled his soda?"

Blank, exhausted stares looked back at him. He kept going.

"That wasn't an accident." Cory smiled dumbly. "That was *on porpoise*."

Skunk cracked the tiniest smile.

"What's a dolphin's favorite TV game show?" Cory looked from one member of his team to the next. He didn't wait for a response: "*Whale* of Fortune."

Preeti groaned loudly.

"Why did the dolphin cross the beach?" Cory grinned as wide and dumb as he could. "To get to the other *tide*."

"Oh, please stop!" Preeti broke down, smiling as she pleaded.

"Why does a dolphin ask a fish how much he weighs?"

Skunk shook his head.

"Because fish have all the scales!"

"Stop!" Skunk laughed. "We'll do anything! Just make the bad jokes stop!"

"You'll apologize to each other?" Cory asked.

Skunk hesitated, then nodded.

"I'm sorry," Skunk said, through gritted teeth. "I'm glad you're a part of this team."

"I'm sorry, too," Preeti told him. "It's tough to have a team member injured."

They both looked to Cory to see if he was satisfied. Those were the best apologies he was going to get. Neither of them were happy about it, but it was a start. His team was holding up as best they could under the circumstances. Cory folded his hands on the table. "Eat up," he told Skunk, "and then we'll go down to check on Tomas. All of us together. Deal?"

Skunk began to eat. Preeti gave Cory a quick nod.

He couldn't be sure, but he thought she might have just showed him a sign of respect. He'd diffused a dangerous situation, one she had started by being insensitive. Sometimes, Cory realized, leadership wasn't just about giving orders or being the best. Sometimes it was about knowing when to tell a joke, no matter how stupid the joke. Sometimes people just needed to laugh.

When they got back to the cargo bay, however, the veterinarian's news was no laughing matter.

11:
BREAKING THE LAW

THE five dolphin handlers stood in a semicircle in front of Dr. Morris, who had been a veterinarian with the navy's Marine Mammal Program as long as anyone could remember. She had deployed on missions all over the globe to care for the dolphins and sea lions who served with the navy, and though she had seen a lot of animals injured, she had never lost one on her watch. She considered her first duty to the well-being of the marine mammals, and her second to the navy's mission.

The grim look on her face suggested she had failed both.

"Tomas suffered severe internal trauma," she said. "Not only had his lungs collapsed, but he had extensive damage to his intestines, liver, and kidneys. He was in a great deal of pain, and extreme efforts to sustain his life would have only made his suffering worse. We made the decision to let him expire."

"Let him *expire*?" Skunk choked out.

"He passed away during surgery," Dr. Morris clarified. "The others have only minor scrapes, normal for an active dolphin, but Tomas took a direct hit with a sharp object." Her tone changed from sympathetic to stern and official. "I have told command that the other four dolphins are able to return to duty, however, I recommended that they *not* be deployed in a combat situation again, as such use violates rules and laws governing the care and keeping of marine mammals in captivity." She locked eyes with Cory, giving him a look that made it clear how she felt about his order to send the dolphins in to fight. "I will be noting such violations in my official report."

"Yes, Doctor," said Cory.

She used big words, but she was telling him what he already knew. He had broken the law by deliberately sending his dolphins to fight. He also knew, however, that he would never have to face a judge or a jury. He would never be charged with a crime, even though he had committed one. The mission was top secret and the veterinarian's official report would be, too.

Cory would still be punished, though. He would be punishing *himself* for the rest of his life. It was his order that had sent one of the dolphins to his death. It was his fault.

"Can I . . . see Tomas?" Skunk asked. Dr. Morris nodded and Cory moved to join them, but Skunk shook his head. "If it's all the same, Chief, I'd rather do this alone."

"Aye aye, Sailor," Cory said as sympathetically as he could. Skunk just turned away and he and the doctor left the cargo hold together, leaving Cory standing in front of the other handlers.

"Check in with your dolphins," he told them. "And then get some rest."

They nodded and broke apart to visit their own animals.

Cory breathed deep the stink of fish and salt water in the air, laced with the scent of fuel and engine grease that sank its way into everything in the cargo hold. Then he walked to Kaj's pool, moved the netting aside, and climbed up, perching on the small platform so his legs dangled in the water.

Kaj perked up the moment Cory approached, his glassy eyes brightening. He blew a salty breath into the air and then swam to Cory's feet, bumping them playfully beneath the surface. The dolphin had no idea he'd lost a member of his pod. Were he and Tomas friends? Did dolphins *have* friends?

He knew dolphins had memories. They remembered commands. They remembered tricks. They remembered people and places and procedures. And every dolphin also had a name in their own language, a unique pattern of whistles. Dolphins remembered each other's whistle-names after even as long as twenty years without seeing each other. Cory wondered if they missed each other in that time. Did dolphins grieve for each other? Did they mourn when one of them died?

There was so much that science didn't know about these amazing animals. So much Cory didn't know.

And yet still, he'd ordered them to fight.

"Do dolphins forgive?" Cory asked Kaj aloud.

Kaj just stared back at him. His black eyes gave not a single clue as to what he might be thinking, whether he knew Cory's sadness or his regret. Whether he knew that the danger wasn't over and that Cory could not protect him.

He rubbed Kaj's smooth snout, letting the dolphin press the hard bone at the tip up against Cory's palm over and over again. It was almost like a dog nuzzling, except Kaj wasn't a beloved pet. He was an advanced intelligence from under the sea. He was also a valuable military asset.

In Cory's mind, at that moment, those two things contradicted each other.

"Only time I had ever seen dolphins before this

mission was at the aquarium in Baltimore," Lieutenant Majeueski said, suddenly standing beside him. "Amazing creatures."

"Yes, sir." Cory moved to salute him, but the lieutenant waved him off.

"They did tricks in the aquarium," he told Cory. "They're good for a lot more than jumping through hoops, though, huh?"

"Yes, sir, they are," said Cory.

"I know you're hurting right now," the lieutenant said. "But we need you. Briefing in twenty minutes."

"My team's exhausted, sir," Cory said. "In more ways than one. We can't possibly deploy again today. The vet would never clear us, anyway."

"McNab, I don't need your team," the lieutenant said. "Just you."

"Sir?"

"We're working up a plan to neutralize the Russian dolphin program, and we need your help."

"Neutralize?" Cory furrowed his brow.

The lieutenant nodded, but didn't explain.

The navy used words like *neutralize* when what they really meant was "kill."

"I don't know if I can —" Cory began, but the lieutenant cut him off.

"That dolphin killed one of yours," he said.

"He didn't do it out of anger," said Cory. "Dolphins aren't like that. They're not bloodthirsty."

"Neither are soldiers," the officer told him. "I'm a SEAL, which means I am trained to be the tip of the navy's sword on sea, air, and land. I am trained to do violence wherever violence is needed. My *job* is *violence*. You can be pretty sure if my team and I are called up, it's because somebody is gonna get hurt. Does that mean I like violence? That *I'm* bloodthirsty? No. And that dolphin wasn't, either. And neither are you. But the dolphin that the Russians have got? It's trained to kill, and it'll make it so that we can't disarm those mines without risking more lives. And if one of those mines blows apart a ship, there'll be even more death. So a dolphin has to be put down because it's dangerous, like a rabid dog. That's what we need you to do. Help us put it down."

"But why me?"

"Because you know how to handle dolphins, and you've been on covert operations before," the lieutenant told him. "And after the order you just gave to deploy those dolphins today, we know you can take extraordinary measures when extraordinary measures are called for."

Cory stood up straight, defiant. "I am under no obligation to follow immoral orders."

"Immoral?" The lieutenant shook his head, laughed. "Are you a philosopher now?"

"I just don't think I can kill an innocent dolphin, sir," Cory said.

"Innocent?" The Lieutenant frowned. "Does that mean there can be a guilty dolphin?"

Cory didn't answer.

"You know, I saw this movie once," the lieutenant continued. "About these Japanese fishermen who kill around two thousand dolphins a year for their meat.

They lure them into a cove and then just chop the dolphins to pieces. You want to fight some moral fight? Fight that. War is messy, and this one dolphin we're after? It's just a casualty of a war." The lieutenant sighed. "You risked your dolphins' lives to keep my guys from risking theirs. You lost one. Now, if we don't eliminate this hostile dolphin before it's deployed against us again, my guys will be at risk and what you did will have been for nothing. One of your dolphins will have died for nothing. What sense does that make?"

Cory flinched. The lieutenant was right. And the lieutenant knew it. He pressed on.

"Listen, McNab, I won't order you to do this, but wouldn't you rather have someone who cares about dolphins put this one down gently?" He met Cory's eyes. "I can promise you, if my guys do it, if any other guys do it, it will not be gentle. They're still angry about the divers we lost and they want revenge. But you? You're the perfect guy for this job. No anger, no malice. Just the knowledge that war's strange and bloody and sometimes we have to do terrible things to keep worse from being done."

"You know, sir," Cory said at last, "you're the one who sounds like a philosopher now."

The lieutenant smiled sadly. "I studied philosophy in college, actually," he said. "Never thought I'd use it like this, to convince a sailor to assassinate a dolphin with me." He shook his head. "You ready to go to the briefing room?"

"Yes, sir," Cory told him. He looked back at Kaj, who'd popped his face out of the water to watch the conversation. "But I have some suggestions for how this needs to go down."

"*That*, McNab, is *exactly* what we need you for. You're the expert."

"I never thought I'd use my expertise like this."

The lieutenant patted his shoulder. As they left the cargo hold together, Cory's heart pounded against his chest. He would go on this mission, but he had his own idea about what would happen on it.

He wasn't going to kill the enemy dolphin. He was going to steal it.

He'd broken the law once already today, so, he figured, why not add treason to the list of his crimes? He just had to figure out how to do it without getting caught.

Or getting killed himself.

12:
SILENT AND DEADLY

THAT night, the mission deployed on two ink-black inflatable boats onto an ink-black sea in the ink-black night. The boats — dubbed "combat rubber raiding crafts," or CRRCs — were smaller than the rigid-hull inflatable boats that the dolphin handlers used. They sat lower in the water and were the favorite of Navy SEALs on covert shore missions.

Their engines ran quiet; their communications were silent. They were invisible.

Each small boat had a four-man recon team of SEALs on board. There was a driver, a sniper, a medic, and another guy who could serve as jack-of-all-trades as the mission demanded. The snipers carried FN MK 20 Sniper Support Rifles with Nightforce scopes, while the others were armed with silenced MP5 submachine guns. Lieutenant Majeueski was the mission commander, and he was with Cory in one of the boats.

Cory had a silenced pistol strapped to his leg and a syringe in a pouch on his chest. The syringe had been filled with a powerful toxin. It was attached to a small CO_2 cartridge. When the needle was injected through the tough skin of a dolphin, the CO_2 would fire the poison deep into the dolphin's flesh with tremendous force.

There was just enough toxin in the syringe to paralyze the Russian dolphin. Once injected, it would stop the unfortunate animal from being able to swim. The dolphin wouldn't be able to surface in order to breathe, and so it would simply drown. By the time the dolphin's body would be recovered, the toxin would be out of its blood, and it would look to any Russian veterinarians who examined the dolphin as if it had drowned by accident, which sometimes happens to dolphins in captivity.

The plan was as clever as it was cruel.

Cory had no intention of following through with it.

But he couldn't just refuse the order. Like the lieutenant had said, the navy would simply have found someone else to do it.

If he was going to keep the Russian dolphin alive, but also keep it from hurting any other US Navy divers, Cory would have to get it away from the port. He couldn't just set the dolphin free, though. It would still be a threat to the US Navy divers, and it would probably return to its handler, anyway. Just like the American-trained dolphins, all that this one dolphin knew was a life in captivity, being fed and cared for by humans. It would never survive in the wild.

The only thing Cory could do was kidnap it.

But how did you kidnap a dolphin?

He'd have to sneak past the Russian commandos on the base in order to get to the dolphin's sea pen, then trick the Navy SEAL recon team he was deploying with, and then trick the crew of the USS *McNamara* to take the Russian dolphin on board, and then the entire US Navy so he could get the dolphin safely to the base in San Diego.

He had an idea how to do it, but his plan was *nearly* impossible. If he was going to pull it off, he'd need help. A lot of it.

He'd also need some luck.

As the boats bounced on the waves, speeding toward the Russian naval base, Cory felt a lump of fear in his throat, bigger than his head. So many things could go wrong now.

The mission was so top secret that no one who wasn't directly involved was supposed to know about it. Not even the captain of the USS *McNamara* knew all the details.

But Cory had told some people.

After he had been briefed on the mission, he went to find Skunk. The sailor was lying in his rack, the middle bed in a stack of three, in a narrow corridor that had two other stacks of beds on each side. Nine sailors could be stacked like frozen fish on top of each other. The lights never went off in the corridor and the hum and bustle of the ship never stopped. There were curtains you could close on each bunk, but they did nothing to block out the sound of sailors coming and going at all hours. It was amazing anyone ever got any sleep at all on board the *McNamara*.

Skunk wasn't asleep. He'd left his curtain open and he stared up at the bottom of the rack above him with his hands clasped behind his head on the pillow. His streak of white hair practically glowed in the shadow of his bed. There were straps along the outside of the bunk to keep a sleeper from rolling out in rough seas, but Skunk hadn't snapped them shut, either. They hung like tentacles from the bed.

"You should get some rest, Chief," Skunk said without looking at Cory. "You look about as fresh as a bucket of fish left out in the sun."

Cory snorted a laugh.

"Do you need me, Chief, or can I go back to my rest

and relaxation?" Skunk said without any humor in his voice.

"I need to talk to you," Cory said.

"But I don't feel much need to talk to you," Skunk said. "So unless you've got an official order for me, I'm not on duty again for five more hours. Until I am on duty, would you mind leaving me alone, please?"

"I'm sorry," said Cory. "I'm sorry for what happened to Tomas. I had no choice."

"There's always a choice." Skunk sighed. "Only one who didn't have a choice was Tomas."

"I understand," said Cory. "I'm sick about it myself, but what's done is done. I had to save the lives of our divers. I had to save the lives of the SEALs who were about to go into the water themselves. So yes, I made a choice and that choice cost Tomas his life."

Skunk didn't say anything.

"You know why I became a dolphin handler?" Cory asked Skunk. "I was surfing with my little brother this one time, and a shark attacked us. Ripped a chunk out of my brother's side. I tried to punch that shark off my brother and it nearly drowned me. I mean, we were done for. Except a pod of wild dolphins chased that shark away and pushed both of us toward shore. I owe my life and my brother's life to dolphins. I don't take hurting them lightly, and I'll never forgive myself for what happened to Tomas. I'm not asking you to forgive me, either. But I need your help now to save another dolphin from meeting the same fate he did."

Skunk sat up on his elbows. He cocked his head. He was listening.

"It isn't one of our dolphins," Cory added. "It's the one who attacked us. The one who killed Tomas." Skunk took a deep breath. Cory continued. "If I'm going to save him, I'll need you to handle Kaj for me. Tonight."

Skunk swung his legs out of his bunk and sat up, leaning forward. "Now I'm really listening."

Cory glanced around the corridor, making sure all the other bunks were empty. He didn't want anyone else hearing what he was about to say. "It's not exactly an authorized mission I'm giving you, and it is very much *un*-authorized that I tell you what I'm about to tell you."

"Hey, you're Chief Petty Officer Cory McNab," said Skunk. "If you authorize it, then it's as authorized as I need it to be."

Cory told him the orders he'd received to kill the Russian dolphin, and his own secret plan to save the dolphin instead. He laid his plan out in detail, or in as much detail as he was comfortable giving Skunk. He wanted to leave Skunk some room to deny knowing that Cory's decision wasn't approved by command if they were caught or if the plan went wrong. Not that Cory thought Skunk would deny it, but he should have that choice, at least.

When he was done, Skunk was on his feet, pulling his blue camo utilities on.

"You sure you're okay with this?" Cory asked him once more.

"I'm the most okay I've been since this thing started," Skunk said. "But how are you going to get

Preeti to go along? Anything happens to you, she's in charge of the Mark Sixty dolphin program. You know she'd like that."

Cory nodded. "She's also the best handler we've got —"

"Don't sell yourself short, Chief," Skunk said. Cory felt himself smile. A compliment from Skunk, who had no reason to compliment him. It was a small gesture, but it told him they'd begun to heal.

"She's a trained Special Warfare Combatant-craft Operator," said Cory. "If my plan's gonna work, we'll need her."

"Good luck convincing her," said Skunk, pulling on his boots.

"Well . . ." said Cory. "I'm going to need *you* to do that, after we deploy. I don't want to say anything to her until the operation is under way."

"In case she reports you?"

Cory nodded.

"You know she doesn't like me very much?" Skunk said.

"I have confidence you'll think of some way to convince her," said Cory. "And I'll need you to talk to Dr. Morris, too. She won't listen to me right now."

"Aye aye," said Skunk. "I think she'll be glad to hear about this . . . even if it could get us all dragged before a court-martial and thrown in prison for treason."

"If we pull this off, no one will get court-martialed," he said.

"And if we don't pull this off?"

Cory cleared his throat. "Let's just make sure we do."

As Cory turned to leave, Skunk whispered after him. "Saving this dolphin's life doesn't make up for Tomas, you know? It doesn't bring him back."

"I know," said Cory. "But we're on the edge of a war, and I'm just trying to save whatever lives I can."

13:
STRIKE PHASE

THE driver of Cory's boat cut the engines half a mile from their target location. The lieutenant put his finger to his ear and listened to some update from command that no else could hear. Cory held his breath. If Skunk hadn't gotten Preeti to go along with his secret plan and if she had reported him, then the lieutenant would probably be getting an order to end the mission and place Cory under arrest.

Instead, the lieutenant nodded and spoke into their shared intercom, which everyone could hear over their earpieces. "We've got the green light," he said. "Time to get in the water."

Cory lifted the regulator attached to the tank on his back and put it in his mouth. With a thumbs-up, he rolled backward off the side of the little boat and sank below the dark surface with barely a splash. The lieutenant, the medic, and one more SEAL followed. The driver and the sniper would stay on the boat, and the SEALs on the other boat would wait to provide backup if needed.

The strike phase of their mission had begun, right on time.

Cory said a silent prayer that Skunk had his plan under way back on the *McNamara*. He had no way to know if it was happening, but he'd find out soon enough. If Skunk didn't show when he was supposed to, the Russian dolphin would be dead. Cory might be, too, by that point.

But those were worries for later. For now, he had a long swim ahead.

The water was black, and it was only through his narrow night-vision lens that he could see anything at all. The other SEALs fanned out around him, and they all swam off with the lieutenant in the lead.

Their tanks were the "rebreather" kind, which had one hose going in, carrying air when the diver inhaled, and another hose going out that collected the breath when they exhaled. Not only did that mean they produced no bubbles, which would rise to the surface and give away the SEALs' location, it also allowed them to stay underwater longer because the tank scrubbed and recycled every breath they took. As long as they didn't dive too deep, they could stay underwater for hours.

Cory hoped they wouldn't have to. Even with his wet suit on, the Black Sea was cold, like swimming through a glass of ice water. After a few minutes, he even considered peeing in his wet suit to stay warm. It was a gross thought, but half of all scuba divers did it . . . and Cory suspected the other half only pretended they didn't.

He decided not to, though. Who wanted to go on a

long, cold swim on a top-secret mission sloshing around in a pee-filled wet suit? Not Cory, that was for sure.

As they swam, big fish darted through Cory's field of vision and his mind played tricks on him, imagining shapes in the dark, just past where he could see. He conjured the shadows of massive sharks, whole schools of them skulking overhead, but the moment he looked up, the shadows would dissolve. It was a moonless night, and there was of course no light below the ocean to cast shadows. Cory marveled at how the imagination could be such a powerful, spooky thing.

The other divers looked a bit spooked, too. Their heads darted a little too quickly toward any movement; their practiced swimming seemed just a touch more frantic than it should've. They were probably wondering the same thing as Cory: What would happen if the Russian dolphin was out of its pen, on patrol? What would happen if that dolphin found them with the kill dart attached to its snout? Would Cory and his syringe be able to save them?

Cory knew the answer already. If they encountered the enemy dolphin in open water, they were dead. Like he'd told the lieutenant, there was no outsmarting a dolphin in its element, and no outswimming it. The divers were completely vulnerable. The best they could do was stay near large objects, like buoys and piers and the seafloor. That still wouldn't be able to trick a dolphin's bio-sonar, but it at least made them feel like they were doing something to protect themselves.

As they swam, Cory went over the plans in his mind.

The official plan was to sneak into the naval base with the SEALs, locate the dolphin pen, slip into the water, and inject the dolphin with the paralyzing toxin, then swim the half mile back out to the boats again. If all went well, there wouldn't be a single shot fired or a single noise made. Their legs would be sore from all that swimming, but it'd be mission accomplished.

The unofficial plan — Cory's plan — was another matter entirely. Up until giving the injection it was exactly the same, but from that moment on it would be a question of daring, luck, skill, and timing. He'd need Skunk and Preeti to do their part based only on Skunk's word. He'd need Dr. Morris to take a big risk and tell an even bigger lie, and he'd need the SEALs not to figure out what he was up to in time to stop him.

Cory went over every anxious step in his mind, and found that the intense thinking passed the time. He could even forget the cold water, the burning in his leg muscles, and the terrible fear churning in his stomach. Before he knew it, he and the other divers had assembled, just below the water's surface, at the end of a long pier at the Russian naval base in Sevastopol.

The lieutenant signaled for one of his SEALs to have a look around. He used a tiny handheld periscope to check out the situation above the waterline, then gave the all-clear sign. One at a time, the team climbed out of the water, ditched the regulators from their mouths, and switched their guns off of safety.

Cory was the last to surface. He scurried along the pier, moving silently, communicating with the SEALs in gestures, just like he did with dolphins. Watching them move, he figured that Navy SEALs and dolphins were similar in a lot of ways. They were fast, powerful, and perfectly suited to their environment.

The team gathered again behind a rusty forklift, just as they heard the sound of Russian commandos approaching. One of them laughed at something the other said. Cory unholstered his silenced pistol, closed his eyes. The commandos kept walking and the night fell silent once again.

"Yo, Chief," the SEAL lieutenant beside him whispered. "You can't shoot with your eyes closed. Open up."

Cory opened his eyes and made his move, creeping away from the cover of the forklift. The SEAL team followed, and as soon as Cory had located the dolphin pen, he and one of the SEALs went back into the water. While the others waited on the pier, Cory slipped into the killer dolphin's watery pen.

The moment the Russian dolphin saw him, Cory's secret phase of the mission began. This was the phase where his plans took a different direction, the phase where he couldn't afford any mistakes. This was the phase where he found himself underwater with a six-hundred-pound dolphin charging at him . . . and both he and the dolphin had been trained to kill each other.

14:
BREAK IN, BREAK OUT

THE Russian dolphin didn't have the kill dart on in its pen, but its bite could cause serious injury without any man-made weapon attached, and being rammed by a dolphin's snout was enough to kill a shark, let alone a skinny bag of bones like Cory.

Cory held the syringe up and ready. The SEAL had attached a blade to the end of his gun and hovered, just on the other side of the underwater netting, prepared to slice the dolphin open if Cory missed his injection.

Cory couldn't afford to miss, for his sake, the SEAL's, or the dolphin's.

The dolphin came at him fast out of the darkness. With one flick of its tail, it shot at him like nature's torpedo. Its gray skin glowed green in the night-vision scope. As it approached, it opened its mouth, showing the jaw of small sharp teeth, then snapped its mouth shut again, making a loud cracking sound under the water. This was the dolphin's warning, trying to scare Cory off.

Just before it hit Cory, it turned, knocking him back against the underwater fence with the side of its body.

The regulator popped from Cory's mouth as the air was knocked from his lungs in a scream of bubbles. The dolphin disappeared into the murky water at the back of its pen once more.

It didn't pass through the cut in the fence to escape, nor did it go in for the kill on Cory.

Cory scrambled to get the breathing apparatus back in his mouth before he himself drowned. The mouthpiece was filled with water and he didn't have enough air left to clear it by exhaling, like he normally would. Instead, he pressed the purge button on its side and a blast of air released from the tank, clearing the mouthpiece of water. As he gasped for a desperate breath, Cory realized he'd made a big mistake.

The bubbles from the purge button rose through the water.

They hit the surface and broke apart in rings. Anyone watching from the guard tower above would see the bubbles and know there were divers below, divers in the water where they should not be.

Cory froze.

Maybe, he thought, the bubbles hadn't been seen. Maybe no one was looking as they broke apart on the surface in perfectly unnatural rings. Maybe he'd gotten lucky.

A spotlight burst on, lighting the water all around him as bright as day.

He hadn't gotten lucky.

The SEAL outside the fence made an agitated gesture across his throat, telling Cory to stick his syringe in the dolphin right now. They were out of time. Under the glare of the spotlights, the divers were completely visible from the surface.

Cory swam forward. The dolphin — alarmed by the lights — swam up to Cory and knocked into him with its snout. A full-force hit from the dolphin could've broken Cory's ribs, ruptured his lungs, or killed him in any number of ways. But the dolphin hadn't wanted to hurt him. It had to know that handlers came in to train and to play, so it wouldn't attack while inside its pen. The aggressive snap of its jaws was just the dolphin's way of testing Cory; bumping him was just curiosity. It wasn't on duty, and until it was, it wouldn't attack.

It wasn't in a dolphin's nature to kill people indiscriminately. It had to be instructed to go after a swimmer . . . instructed by a human to do what it wouldn't do naturally.

Cory figured that there must be a series of signals that this dolphin's handlers gave to let it know when it was time to become a lethal weapon. As long as it never received that signal, it wouldn't be a danger to Cory or the divers. It wasn't the dolphin that was an enemy of the navy, it was the dolphin's handlers.

But there was no time to explain that to the SEAL making a throat-slitting gesture at Cory, ordering him to do his job immediately. There was no time to explain anything, actually.

Bullets sliced into the water around them, hundreds of streaks tracing deadly paths all around Cory and the SEAL. They slashed through the water close to the dolphin, too. The rebel commandos who controlled the base fired their machine guns into the water wildly. They lacked training and discipline, but not bullets. They might kill their own dolphin while trying to kill the intruders. Even underwater, Cory could hear the pop and crack of the guns. He worried the sea would soon have more lead in it than salt.

The SEAL swam forward, his blade up. If Cory wasn't going to execute the dolphin so they could get out of the line of fire, he would.

Cory gestured for him to stay back. He raised the syringe, turned the knob on the small CO_2 tank, and, just as the Russian dolphin turned to investigate what Cory had in his hand, he jabbed down with it, injecting it into the top of the dolphin's head, just behind its blowhole, where the paralyzing toxin would reach its brain the most quickly.

Except there was no paralyzing toxin in the syringe.

Before the mission, Cory had switched the syringe of poison for one filled with Dr. Morris's dolphin vitamin formula. He'd tossed the actual poison into the incinerator of the USS *McNamara*.

The dolphin twisted and thrashed when the needle jabbed it. It spun away and dove, nearly smacking Cory's head off with the sweep of its tail fin. The needle broke away from its tough skin and sank, and Cory held up his hand for the SEAL to see. He signaled that the job was done. Just then, the spotlight shut off and the machine-gun fire ceased.

Less than thirty seconds had passed, but it felt like hours.

The SEAL sniper at sea had shot out the spotlight.

The SEALs on the pier, Cory knew from the brief-ing, would have opened fire from silenced machine guns, forcing commandos to take cover while the SEALs fell back one by one, firing and moving, firing and moving.

The SEAL with Cory motioned for him to swim out of the pen again. By the time he had, the others had rejoined them in the dark water, and they all swam like mad along the seafloor for the CRRCs, which were moving closer to keep up cover fire and evacuate the divers.

Once they were under their CRRC, the SEALs moved straight up for the surface, popping on board one at a time, as fast as they could. Once Cory had sur-faced, he looked back to the pier. Commandos scurried from place to place, shouting at each other, trying to see where the attackers had gone, not knowing they'd already swum from the port. The snipers took occa-sional shots from the front of the boats to force the commandos to keep their heads down. If they couldn't come out from under cover, they couldn't board their own boats to give chase. That would give the SEALs enough time to get away.

Except, in order for Cory's plan to work, they couldn't get too far away. He needed the dolphin to chase them. He needed the Russian dolphin handler to *make* the dolphin chase them. He watched the pier through his night-vision goggles while he waited for the last SEAL diver to get out of the water, and he murmured a silent prayer to himself.

With enemy divers in the water, the smart choice would be to deploy their dolphin. That's what Cory would do in their position. That's what Cory hoped they would do.

And then, as if in answer to his prayers, one figure came out from the cover of a shipping container and scurried for the edge of the dock around the dolphin's pen. Cory saw the dolphin surface and the handler begin to signal it to find the underwater intruders.

"I've got movement near the dolphin pen," the sniper on Cory's boat said.

The lieutenant looked through his scope, seeing the same thing as Cory. The dolphin popped half out of the water, the handler gesturing with instructions.

"I thought you got that dolphin," the lieutenant said.

"I saw him do it," the SEAL who'd been with Cory responded.

"The toxin takes a little bit to work," Cory lied. "The dolphin won't be a threat soon."

"Handler's making moves," the sniper said. Cory watched through his scope as the handler fitted the dolphin with the kill dart. The sniper locked on. "Permission to engage?"

"The dolphin's not a threat," Cory repeated.

"Take out the handler," the lieutenant ordered.

"No," Cory gasped under his breath. The final gesture hadn't been given. The dolphin was still waiting. If they killed its handler before the signal, the dolphin would stay in its pen. The mission would be a failure, and the next time the divers got into the water to disarm the mines, they'd be in just as much danger as before. The only way to protect them would be for Cory to confess that he *hadn't* injected the poison. He'd go to prison and a new team would be sent to assassinate the dolphin. It would've all been for nothing.

"Send it," the lieutenant ordered.

Cory watched in silent horror, as the handler raised his arm in the final *go* gesture, just as the SEAL sniper squeezed the trigger. The Russian handler suddenly dropped like a rag doll, his life extinguished as quick as blowing out a match.

As he fell, his suddenly limp arm fell, too, and the Russian dolphin, with no idea its human partner had just been killed, thought it had gotten the signal. It splashed underwater, disappearing.

"Target down," the sniper said.

"Confirmed," said the lieutenant. "We're clear. Roll out."

With that, both CRRC engines revved, the boats spun, and they began their high-speed race toward their ship, mission accomplished as far as everyone but Cory knew.

On the dock, the commandos boarded speedboats to search their harbor for the intruders.

"I count four boats," the sniper told them, looking through his scope. "Eight men on each. Light machine guns."

The lieutenant must have seen the worry on Cory's face. "Don't worry," he said. "They can't see us and they won't catch up."

But it wasn't the commandos Cory was worried about. Somewhere beneath the roiling sea, an attack dolphin, who was supposed to be dead, was on the hunt for divers it had no way of knowing were long gone, and that it would never be rewarded for finding, anyway.

Its handler was dead.

Cory was its only hope now.

15:
YOU CAN'T GO IT ALONE

CORY bit his lower lip. He checked his dive watch for the time. His dolphin team should be on their way.

They had better be. He was counting on his own dolphin for this crazy plan of his to work. He couldn't do it without Kaj. He looked back toward the navy base. Lights from the two Ukrainian warships blinked and Cory imagined the sailors on board, stuck in harbor, unable to go ashore, wondering when it would be their turn to be boarded, to be taken prisoner, or worse. If the next part of Cory's plan worked, those ships would be safely out of harbor by morning, too, and the Russian commandos would be holding a naval base without any warships and without a trained attack dolphin.

"Movement on our six," one of the SEALs said, raising his weapon and pointing straight off the back of the boat at whatever movement he saw directly behind them.

Cory and the lieutenant looked, but saw nothing, just the wake their boat's outboard engine made cutting the waves. But then a shining shape, dark gray and glistening, leapt from the water, its whole body above the surface. It hung an impossible moment in the air before knifing back below the surface. It sliced along behind them, keeping perfect pace with their boat, even speeding up to swim directly alongside. Its dorsal fin traced a delicate line across the sea, just before it breached again, leaping along next to the SEALs' boat, close enough to touch. Close enough for all of them to see the small tank strapped to its side and the kill dart harnessed to the tip of its snout.

"I thought you hit it, McNab," Lieutenant Majeuski snapped at him. "That dolphin is very much not paralyzed!"

"It . . ." Cory didn't know what to say. Did he admit his trick, try to bring the lieutenant into his scheme? Did he simply lie and say the poison must not have been effective? He needed to say *something*.

The sniper spun around, brought up his SR25 high-powered rifle, and trained it just above the waterline. Cory could see the gentle rise and fall of the barrel as the sniper adjusted for the bounce of their boat and the rolling leaps of the dolphin.

"Target acquired," he said, with deadly calm. He waited. Even as they raced along the waves and the dolphin raced along beside them, the sniper was as still as a statue, the fluid movement of his weapon the only sign that he was tracking his target at all. From this close range, the sniper could blast a hole clear through the Russian dolphin's brain the instant it broke the surface. It would be a painless death, much more humane than the paralyzing poison would have been. Perhaps

Cory should just let the sniper fire. Perhaps this was as close as a war dolphin could get to mercy: a quick death in the water, as opposed to being torn from the only sea it knew and taken away from its home forever.

How had right and wrong become so blurry when life and death were so clear? Perhaps this was what people meant when they used the phrase "fog of war." His head felt foggy thinking about it all.

The lieutenant looked at Cory, eyebrows furrowed, as he considered giving the order for his sniper to fire. He cocked his head slightly. "Hold," he said slowly.

The sniper held the target in his sights but didn't shoot.

"You didn't inject the poison into that dolphin, did you?" the lieutenant asked.

"Your guy saw me do it," Cory told him.

"My guy saw you inject something," said the lieutenant. "But I read up on what should've happened with the dosage of poison you were using. No way that dolphin's swimming right now if there was really poison in your syringe."

The boat driver kept driving, the rear gunner kept his gun up, scanning the horizon for threats, and the sniper kept his rifle locked on the dolphin swimming beside them. However, all of them were listening to their officer confront Cory, who realized more than ever at that moment that he was an outsider, not a Navy SEAL, and he was on *their* boat, on *their* mission, and his decision had put them *and* their mission at risk. There was no way out of this; there were no more lies to tell. Truth was the only path he had in front of him, but it was also the riskiest path. Covert operations didn't lend themselves to honesty, but if there was any way to save this dolphin's life, honesty was the way to find it.

"Send it," the lieutenant said.

"Wait!" Cory cried out.

"Hold!" the lieutenant barked. The sniper's finger paused on the trigger, about to squeeze. "You gonna tell me what's going on now?" the lieutenant asked Cory.

"We can't kill that dolphin," Cory said.

"We have to," said the lieutenant. "You and I have been over this."

They could hear the loud engines of the Russian speedboats crisscrossing the water and the commandos shouting to each other, in the distance but getting closer. The area was so large, there was no way they could find the SEALs in the dark, and yet they seemed to be zeroing in. That's when Cory realized there was a tracking device on the dolphin swimming beside them. The dolphin was leading the enemy right to their position!

"There's another way," Cory said. "But we have to move fast and you have to trust me."

"Why should I do that?" the lieutenant asked. "You lied to me, and you endangered the mission. I should have you arrested."

"Our job here was to eliminate the dolphin so we could clear the mines and the warships could get out of port safely, right? To prevent war breaking out?"

The lieutenant nodded.

"My plan saves this dolphin and those ships," Cory continued. "I knew you'd never agree to it ahead of time, but it's the best chance we've got of succeeding in all our objectives now."

"You thought you could just go it alone?" Lieutenant Majeuski said. "That is not how we operate, McNab."

"I understand, sir," Cory answered. "And I apologize."

The boat bobbed on the waves. If the lieutenant didn't go along with this, all the apologies in the world wouldn't save Cory now.

"Sir," the radio crackled; the SEALs on the other boat were calling. "You've got hostiles approaching from five and seven o'clock, coming up fast on you."

"Roger that," said the lieutenant. He looked at his sniper, then back at Cory, his lips pursed, thinking.

He checked his watch again.

"We've got movement coming in from twelve o'clock now," the radio crackled.

"In front of us?" the lieutenant's eyes widened. "How'd they get in front of us?"

"Sir," said Cory. "That's my team. Mark Sixty. They're coming to help."

"What have you done?" the lieutenant whispered.

"Please," Cory begged. "Trust me on this."

The lieutenant took a deep breath, then turned to his sniper again. He looked at the Russian dolphin, leaping playfully alongside their boat.

"Stand down," the lieutenant ordered.

"Sir?" The sniper didn't move. His finger was steady on the trigger.

"McNab here saved our skin from this dolphin yesterday," the lieutenant said. "We can give him a chance to save the dolphin's skin from us today."

"Thank you, sir," said Cory.

"Now tell me what you've got in mind," said the lieutenant. "But know that if it falls apart, I'm still putting a bullet in that dolphin and handcuffs on you."

"Understood," said Cory. "Get my team on the radio. We don't have a lot of time."

16:
TRUST AND TRAINING

"**THIS** is Mark Two," Preeti's voice came over the radio, filling Cory's ear with the sweetest sound imaginable: the sound of his team. Skunk had done his job. "I've got Skunk and Kaj with me. And the other . . . *item* . . . as instructed."

"It's good to hear your voice, Sailor," Cory responded.

"You better know what you're doing, Chief," she said.

"Cut the chatter," the SEAL lieutenant interrupted. "This is Viper One Actual. I'm handing over operational control to the Mark Sixty team." He got off the radio and looked at Cory. "Do your thing, Chief, and do it fast. Those hostiles are closing in."

"Roger that," Cory answered, then he got back on the radio. "This is Mark One Actual. Send Kaj to my position." He then told the lieutenant to cut the engine. "I need a few minutes," he said.

"Give us some room, guys," the lieutenant told the other boat. Without hesitation, the other SEALs turned 180 degrees and sped to intercept the commandos' boats and lure them away, drawing their fire. The pop of machine guns grew quieter by the second. The commandos probably thought they were chasing ill-equipped Ukrainian army regulars. They had no idea they were in hot pursuit of armed-to-teeth Navy SEALs, who look forward to open water combat the way baseball players look forward to their turn at bat. A few wild gunshots in the air weren't going to scare them off.

Meanwhile, the Russian dolphin circled Cory's boat.

"Uh, Chief," Skunk's voice came over the comm. "I'm looking at you now, but, uh, the dolphin by your boat has a . . . has a kill dart. We can't send Kaj out."

"I'll have that off in time," Cory said. "Just send Kaj."

"I don't know if —" Skunk said, but Preeti's voice cut him off, all business.

"Kaj on his way," she said.

In the distance, Cory heard the splash of a large animal jumping into the water. His partner was on his way to him. He bent down over the side of the boat and slapped the surface of the water, hoping the Russian dolphin had been trained the same way as the American ones.

Sure enough, the dolphin popped up by the side of the boat, the needle on its nose gleaming. The SEALs turned their guns, aiming straight at the enemy dolphin's head, fingers on the triggers.

"We're cool," Cory said. "No worries." He spoke as calmly as he could, bending down to pat the dolphin. He carefully reached toward the strap around the dolphin's snout to remove the kill dart.

The dolphin knocked his arm away, hard enough that it was going to leave a bruise, but it didn't swim away. Instead, it opened its mouth wide, the long jaw studded with sharp teeth, top and bottom, glistening white. The teeth had been well cared for by the Russian trainers. They were all there, all sharp.

Cory wasn't in the water, so the dolphin didn't think he was a target. It didn't snap its jaws shut. Cory needed this dolphin to think *he* was its handler if he was going to be able to get the dart and CO_2 tank off and give the dolphin new orders. It needed to trust Cory . . . which meant Cory needed to trust it.

Cory took a deep breath and reached out his hand, putting it in the Russian dolphin's mouth to scratch its tongue. If the dolphin didn't trust Cory, it could snap its jaws shut and bite his hand clean off at the wrist.

"Woohee," the SEAL sniper gasped, watching Cory's hand inside the dolphin's jaws.

Over the water, they heard the gunfire in the dark, getting closer again. The flash of tracer fire showed the gunshots snapping back and forth. The commandos were firing at the other SEALs. The SEALs weren't aiming for the commandos, though. They were taking out the engines on the enemy boats. That would give Cory a little more time to do what he needed to do next.

The dolphin let him scratch its tongue with his right hand. With his left, he carefully loosened the strap on the harness around the dolphin's snout and slipped the dart off, then reached farther over the side, toward the dolphin's fin, to take off the CO_2 tank.

Once the weapon was off the dolphin, he dropped the harness into their boat, stopped scratching the tongue, and he lifted his arm up, just like he'd seen the recently departed Russian dolphin handler do. The dolphin sank back lower in the water with its head up and eyes fixed on Cory.

Suddenly, Kaj popped up beside him, lighter gray and smaller than the Russian dolphin. His eyes, too, fixed on Cory. Both dolphins stared and waited. They didn't react to each other the way they would've if they were wild dolphins meeting, especially wild dolphins who had fought each other before. Both of them had been trained to pay attention to humans first. It was exactly the thing that made them different from other dolphins. It was what would allow Cory to save them.

It also helped that dolphins didn't hold grudges.

Cory motioned for the dolphins to wait, which was a universal gesture: palm open with four fingers slightly bent and the index finger raised. The dolphins waited.

So far, so good, Cory thought.

He pulled out the small bag he'd secured in the CRRC, and removed two of the plunger devices they used to have the dolphins mark undersea mines. Then he removed small blocks of C-4 explosive and attached them to the plungers, inserting remote detonator charges into each. All the dolphin team members were trained explosives technicians, and Cory knew how to handle bombs like this.

"You brought explosives onto my boat without telling me?" the lieutenant said to him.

"Sorry, LT," Cory replied. "Add it to the list of my many transgressions."

The lieutenant seethed, but kept his mouth shut. He'd already made the decision to trust Cory and follow his crazy plan. He let Cory do his work.

Cory attached one of the bombs to the Russian dolphin's snout, then turned to Kaj and slipped one on his.

"Be careful, friend," he said, patting Kaj on the head.

He returned to the arm-up position, then made the gestures to instruct Kaj to locate an undersea mine and attach his plunger. Kaj didn't know he was planting a bomb. He thought this was like any other "quick find" drill. He flipped around and disappeared into the sea to do his job.

The Russian dolphin just stared at Cory. Cory stared back at it.

"Oh, come on!" Cory cried out.

"Problem, Chief?" The lieutenant wanted to know what was going on.

"The Russians have different gestures for their dolphins, I guess," he said. "I don't know how to tell this one to do what I need."

The Russian dolphin sank under the boat, swam around, and popped up again, the explosive still on its snout. Cory feared it might plant the bomb on their hull.

"This isn't going to work unless I can tell him what to do."

"Viper One, this is Viper Two," the other CRRC called. "We took out the engines on two of their boats, but you've got two more coming your way. Ten minutes out."

"Roger that, Viper Two," said the lieutenant. "McNab, they are zeroing in on that harness." He pointed to the kill dart and tank, which had the tracking device on it. "Toss it overboard."

"Negative, sir," said Cory. "We're going to need it."

"When, McNab?" the lieutenant asked. "We've got ten minutes."

"Soon, sir," said Cory.

Suddenly, Kaj was back, the plunger gone. Cory patted him, then pulled another from the bag and attached it to Kaj. He gave his dolphin the same gesture. Kaj hesitated, then disappeared again.

With only one dolphin planting the devices, there was no way they'd be done in time. He needed the Russian dolphin to do something.

He repeated the motion. The dolphin just stared at him.

Then, a dark shape moved below, coming right to the other dolphin's tail and bumping it.

The dolphin, startled, dove to investigate and Cory saw Kaj, with plunger and C-4 still attached, harassing the Russian dolphin, snapping at its tail.

"Kaj, what are you doing?" Cory said aloud.

He watched the two dolphins tangle near the surface. The Russian dolphin would try to move for the boat and Kaj would hit it with his whole body, knocking it down, twirling around it, trying to steer it away.

"They fighting?" the lieutenant asked. Cory's memory flashed an image of Tomas, bleeding, having a seizure, dying because of this dolphin's attack. Except now, instead of a needle attached to its snout, it had enough explosives to blow both dolphins and the small boat above them into vapor. None of them would survive this brawl.

"They're . . . uh . . ." Cory had no idea what was happening. He'd never seen Kaj act like this before. Every time the Russian dolphin tried to turn, Kaj blocked it with his body. When the dolphin tried to ram Kaj, Kaj dodged. But then he returned, kept trying to steer the other dolphin.

"You want me to take him out?" the sniper asked.

"Hold," Cory said, worried for Kaj's life, but not ready to give up yet.

The sniper switched his scope, aimed into the water. "No shot," he said, lifting his head away from the rifle. "I don't know which fish is the one on our side."

"Dolphins aren't fish," said Cory. "And they don't choose sides."

"Lost 'em, anyway," the sniper grunted. "They dove too deep."

17:
OLD DOLPHIN, NEW TRICKS

KAJ didn't have the camera attached to his fin, so there was no way for Cory to know what was going on underwater. He feared the next time he saw his dolphin it would be when Kaj's body floated to the surface, or when an underwater explosion blasted him into the air in gruesome pieces.

But instead, just twenty yards off their starboard bow, both dolphins surfaced to breathe side by side and then dove again in unison. They surfaced again, together, and dove again, together.

"They bury their grudge?" the lieutenant asked.

"Dolphins don't hold grudges," said Cory, in wonder. *What did just happen?*

A minute later, both dolphins were back, heads up out of the water beside the boat, looking like mirror images of each other. Cory squinted at them, but their mysterious smiles gave no answers. They had both planted their bombs. They both simply awaited further instructions.

Cory attached the last two of his explosive-carrying devices to them and waved them off to attach them to undersea mines. Kaj dove first and the other dolphin hesitated. Kaj circled back under the water and bumped the other one with his snout, and the dolphin dove after him. They disappeared together.

Cory remembered a video he'd seen on the Internet of a pod of wild dolphins in the Caribbean who used seashells gripped in their mouths like shovels, digging through the hard ocean floor to stir up clams and mussels without scraping their snouts. When researchers took one of these tool-using dolphins and introduced it into a different pod of dolphins, they discovered that the dolphin could actually teach the technique to that new pod. No one told the wild dolphins how to teach each other. They just did it. Like humans, dolphins appeared to have a desire to share their knowledge with each other.

Kaj must have taught the other dolphin what Cory was asking it to do!

In a way, Kaj had just translated between Cory and the other dolphin because they didn't speak the same language. He had understood what Cory wanted and found a way to make the other dolphin understand. How could he strap explosives to such amazing creatures without their knowledge? How could he make them fight in human wars? The pang of guilt tore at Cory.

The sound of approaching boat engines made Cory abandon his thoughts. He looked to the water, waiting for the dolphins to come back.

The moment they popped their heads above the waterline, he called up Preeti on the radio. "Meet me at the following coordinates," he said, and transmitted a location to them and to the other SEAL boat.

"That's right in the middle of a cluster of undersea mines we marked," Preeti said.

"Affirmative," Cory replied. He nodded at their driver, who revved the engines. Cory slapped the water, and the dolphins followed in their wake as they raced toward the spot where he'd just had both of them attach their little bombs to the much much bigger bombs underwater.

"What in the world do you have planned here, McNab?" the lieutenant asked.

"We're going to lure the commandos after us," he said. "And when they're close enough, we're going to blow the whole area sky high. That'll clear a safe path out of harbor for those warships."

"What about the commandos who come after to investigate?" the lieutenant asked.

"Don't worry, LT," Cory told him. "All they'll find is some of their own boat wreckage and the body of one dead dolphin with a tracking device on it."

The lieutenant looked surprised. "After all this, you're still going to kill that dolphin?"

"I didn't say that," Cory told him.

He didn't really want to say exactly what the last part of his plan was. It was better just to do it and get it over with than to talk about it. It wasn't something he'd be proud to do, but he figured saving the day wasn't always pretty or heroic like in the movies. Sometimes, saving the day meant doing the thing no one else wanted to do.

In this case, saving the day meant blowing up a dolphin.

18:
BURIAL AT SEA

THE two inflatable CRRCs met up with the dolphin handlers in their rigid-hull boat. Skunk and Preeti both wore dark-blue pixel-camouflage utilities, the closest thing they had to the black gear that covert operators wore. As Cory had instructed, it was just the two of them on board. Preeti drove and Skunk assisted her and looked after the dolphin equipment.

"Everybody ready on board the *McNamara*?" Cory asked.

"Dr. Morris and her team are standing by," said Preeti. "Cruz and Tully are ready to load the dolphins on board double-time."

Cory took a deep breath. No going back now. The Russian commandos were coming up on them. Tracer fire streaked over the water in the distance.

"They'll be in range soon," said the lieutenant. "Whatever you're going to do, you better do it now."

Cory nodded. He climbed from the CRRC onto the larger boat, bringing the kill dart harness with him. Then he moved to a large tarp tied up on the back of the RHIB. He gave Skunk a lingering glance and Skunk nodded, then looked away.

"I know this wasn't easy," Cory said. "Thank you."

Skunk just cleared his throat and wiped his eyes with the back of his hand.

Cory undid the cords around the tarp, and the material slid open to reveal the gray and lifeless body of Tomas. The curious spark was long gone from his eyes, but the strange dolphin smile remained etched on his face.

"I'm so sorry, Tomas," Cory said aloud, not caring that the others could hear him. "I'm sorry this happened to you. May you swim free in the great beyond, wherever dolphins go when their time on this earth is over."

Those words spoken, Cory took a deep breath and knelt beside Tomas's body. He attached the Russian kill dart to his snout and hooked the tracker and CO_2 tank around his fin the way it had been attached to the Russian dolphin. Then, using the tarp for leverage, he rolled Tomas's body off the back of the boat into the ocean. It bobbed and floated a moment, held up on the surface by the buoyancy of its lifeless blubber and the gas filling the CO_2 tank. The drift of the current began to pull the body away from the boat, and the strange illusion of the waves made it look almost like Tomas was swimming one last time.

Cory exhaled. He saluted the dolphin as he drifted away. Skunk suddenly stood at his side, offering a salute as well. Glancing over his shoulder, Cory saw Preeti and the SEALs from both recon teams saluting, too. It was a fitting good-bye for a navy hero, a burial at sea. Tomas would never know it, but he really was a hero.

Cory fought the urge to flinch with every pop of

machine-gun fire he heard in the distance. The commandos couldn't see them. They were still just firing wildly in the direction of their tracking device. They didn't even know at whom they were shooting. As far as any of them knew, there were no American Special Forces operating in the area.

It was time to make sure they never found out.

Cory snapped off his salute and the others did the same, then he turned to Skunk.

"You ready to do your job again, EOD-3 Reggerio?"

"Ready as I'll ever be, Chief," Skunk said.

"Call Kaj on board, then," said Cory.

"Me?"

"You," Cory told him.

Skunk bent over the side and slapped the water, and Kaj swam to the boat. The other dolphin followed, imitating Kaj move for move. Both had their heads popped out of the water, mouths open. Skunk looked to Cory, who nodded his encouragement. Skunk tossed Kaj a fish from a bucket at his feet, then tossed the Russian dolphin a fish as well.

They each ate their fish in one bite. Skunk made the signal to jump back on board the boat.

Kaj turned and dove below the water, then leapt into the air and slid to a perfect stop on the pad. He bent his tail up and looked from Skunk to Cory, and back to Skunk again.

"Nice job, buddy," said Cory, throwing the dolphin another fish. "Nice job to you too, Skunk."

"Where's the other one?" Preeti asked.

"He's thinking," said Cory, pointing over the side. The Russian dolphin swam in circles around the boat, blowing anxious blasts from its blowhole and eyeing Skunk warily. "Do the motion again," said Cory. "Let's see how quick a learner this guy is."

Skunk repeated the boarding motion and the dolphin dove below. For a moment, Cory feared the dolphin would simply bolt, racing back to port, where the Russians would find it in its pen in the water by the pier.

Instead, the dolphin jumped from the water, just like Kaj had, sliding onto the pad beside him, tail raised toward the sky and mouth wide open. The boat rocked with the weight of two dolphins on the back, but Preeti adjusted the throttle to keep it steady.

"Nice job!" Cory praised the dolphin. Skunk tossed it a fish.

"He did that better than Tomas ever managed," said Skunk.

Cory patted Kaj, then the strange new dolphin. "Skunk, from this moment on, this *is* Tomas."

"Roger that," said Skunk sadly. "Dr. Morris deleted her report on Tomas's death. She'll have new records made up when we get back, just like you said. We just need to add in this dolphin's details."

"You going to be okay?" Cory put his hand on Skunk's back.

Skunk nodded. "As okay as I can be with what we're doing. Faking a dolphin's death and stealing another's identity." He grunted. "So this is the way war is now?"

"This is it," Cory confirmed, sadly.

"Hostiles closing in," the lieutenant announced. "They'll be in range in three minutes."

"I'll see you guys back at the ship," Cory told his team, climbing back aboard the CRRC. "Preeti, drive like a —"

"I know how to exit a hostile environment," Preeti snapped at him, and the moment he was clear of her boat, she spun it and gunned the engines, speeding away to get back to the *McNamara* as fast as possible.

Cory turned to the lieutenant. "Thank you, sir," he said. "That dolphin owes you his life." He pulled the remote detonator for the C-4 explosives from his vest.

"Let's roll," ordered the lieutenant. He waved his finger in the air, and both SEAL boats drove from the path of the oncoming enemy speedboats. Cory watched through the night-vision goggles as the commandos drew closer and closer to Tomas's body and Tomas's body drifted closer and closer to the undersea mines, where Kaj and the Russian dolphin had planted their C-4 explosives.

When the first boat had found the dolphin's corpse and extended a grappling hook to haul it on board, Cory flipped the switch and dropped his thumb on the detonator button.

The ocean exploded.

19:
SMALL FAVORS

THE explosions of C-4 detonated the giant undersea mines that the C-4 was attached to, and those mine explosions set off the mines nearest to them one by one, like dominoes falling. Massive, deadly dominoes.

BOOM. BOOM. BOOM. BOOM.

The sea erupted, bright flashes in the depths. Water shot a hundred feet into the air in terrible geysers. Metal shrapnel whirled and whistled through the night sky, and one of the commandos' boats was ripped to pieces, the men on board thrown into the sea.

The other commando boat steered away, weaving through the bright, blossoming blasts beneath them.

They found themselves racing through an undersea minefield, jumping into the water unarmed to escape when their boat was blasted skyward, too. They'd all given up the chase. They were swimming for shore with all the strength they had left, hauling their wounded with them. The water was foamy and smelled of smoke and ash for miles. Cory surprised himself by hoping they'd all survived the explosion. He didn't think he'd care, but maybe he'd learned something from the dolphins already. Maybe he didn't hold a grudge, either.

"This is Viper One Actual to Mothership." Lieutenant Majeuski spoke into the secure satellite phone as they sped away. "Radio the warships in port. They have a clear path through the mines if they get under way now. Tell them to steer on a heading of . . . well, just tell them to steer straight for those explosions. There's not a mine left. They all detonated."

The lieutenant listened to the response from command, which none of the others could hear. They were no doubt wondering how the mission had changed from eliminating the Russian dolphin to completely clearing the mines, and how those explosions in the Black Sea could ever be explained without admitting that American Special Forces had been involved.

"We were pursued," Lieutenant Majeueski explained. "Our pursuers must have set off their own mines by accident." He smirked at Cory. "They did not identify us."

The lieutenant listened for a moment. "Affirmative," he answered. "Target and handler were eliminated. The Sevastopol dolphin program is inoperative." He paused again. "Roger that. Viper out." He put the receiver back. "Command sends their congratulations on a job well done," he told Cory.

The mission had been a success as far as the officers back on the *McNamara* knew. For the separatist commandos, there would be nothing but wreckage of their own boats left to find, and there would be little of the dolphin's remains left to identify after all those explosions. The survivors would report that they'd found the dolphin just before the mines went off, and they would also report that it had worn the tracking device and kill dart on its snout, just as it had when its handler deployed it, before being shot himself.

The commandos would probably determine that their dolphin had been killed in the explosions while pursuing whatever swimmers had attacked their base. They wouldn't know who had actually staged the attack on their base, but, as Cory had discovered, the "fog of war" left a lot of questions unanswered and a lot of violence unexplained. That was the nature of a covert fight.

The commandos and their Russian backers might suspect the United States of having been involved, but they couldn't prove it. They'd be upset that the warships had slipped out of port, but they'd live to fight another day. They all would.

Neither Cory nor the SEALs nor the United States Navy itself believed they had stopped a war from breaking out between the Russian separatists and the Ukrainian military, but they did know that whatever war between the two nations was to come, neither side would have the use of a trained killer dolphin. The Black Sea was safe from that threat at least, and every threat they eliminated made the world just a tiny bit safer. It wasn't much in a dangerous world, but it was something.

"You covered for me," Cory told the lieutenant. "You made this possible. Thank you."

"You're one crazy fish wrangler," the lieutenant said. "But you got the mission done, Chief, and not one of my guys got hurt. I respect that."

"So can I count on your help when we get back to the ship?" Cory wondered.

"More help, huh?" The lieutenant tapped his fingers against the pistol strapped to his thigh. "You always repay a favor by asking for another favor?"

"It's a small favor this time," Cory said. "I just need you to forget that the Mark Sixty team lost a dolphin yesterday. As far as you know, we deployed five dolphins yesterday and five came back. And tonight, when we needed backup, two of those dolphins were deployed again."

The lieutenant took a deep breath. "So you want me to lie in my official reports, risk my career and maybe face criminal charges if we're caught? And you want everyone on my team out here to do the same?"

"Nothing I wouldn't do myself," Cory said. "In fact, I *am* doing it myself. So is SB-1 Suraj, EOD-3 Reggerio, and our veterinarian, Dr. Morris."

"You'd risk all this to save a dolphin's life?"

Cory nodded. "We save the ones we can. We save the ones who can't save themselves."

The lieutenant exhaled slowly, looking at the water racing by their boat.

"Is that a yes?" Cory asked.

"I'm thinking," the lieutenant said. The SEAL sniper glanced at him curiously. The driver, too. They'd take their cues from their lieutenant, Cory figured. SEAL teammates were like that. They had each other's backs, come what may. Cory was an outsider and he couldn't count on that kind of loyalty from them. Basically, he needed to borrow the loyalty the guys felt for their lieutenant.

Except, when they got back to the *McNamara*, he still hadn't given Cory an answer.

20:
RESTORED TO LIFE

THE docking bay door was open. About a hundred yards out from it, the two SEAL boats lined up next to each other and matched speed. Cory looked across at the other boat. The SEALs had all ducked low, pressing themselves as flat as they could against the inflatable hull. The driver revved the engine. Cory's driver revved his back, and the lieutenant gave a quick shout of the SEAL battle cry:

"Hooyah!"

Both boats gunned their engines and shot forward in the water at full speed.

"Get down, McNab!" the lieutenant yelled at Cory,

yanking him facedown against the bottom of the boat. "You're slowing us down!"

It was a race! They were racing straight for the back of the ship at over thirty knots, and the moment Cory ducked down, cutting the wind resistance pushing them back, their boat pulled ahead. They had a lighter load on board, fewer weapons, and Cory weighed less than the other SEALs.

The boat bounced beneath Cory's face; the water rumbled against the rubber hull like they were driving over hard concrete. Cory turned his head and saw they were just barely in the lead. Neither boat was slowing down. The cargo bay of the *McNamara* loomed large over them. Cory closed his eyes, certain they were about to crash.

At the last moment, the driver cut the engine and spun the boat so that they glided over the submerged loading ramp and slid to a graceful stop inside the wet cargo bay about two whole boat lengths ahead of the other SEALs.

"We have a winner!" the lieutenant declared his boat's victory.

Sailors had gathered all around the cargo bay to cheer the return of the guys from SEAL Team Five. Everyone in the cargo hold burst into applause.

In their mobile tanks, the dolphins of Cory's team popped their bodies from the water, their fins in the air, each of them applauding, too, a trick they'd learned in order to entertain the sailors during transport. Only the dolphin in Tomas's tank didn't applaud, but none of the sailors seemed to notice anything out of the ordinary. To them, all dolphins looked the same. Cory was counting on that. The navy knew it had sent five dolphins overseas, and it was getting five dolphins back. As long as all the paperwork looked right, they would never ask any questions.

When Kaj saw Cory standing in the cargo hold, he flopped backward into his tank and poked his tail above the water. He waved, having a grand old time. He knew he'd done well, even if he didn't know exactly what he had done. And Kaj always figured any applause was for him, even if it wasn't. *It must be a nice way to go through life,* Cory thought.

Dr. Morris, however, wasn't applauding. She strode over to him while the SEALs unpacked their gear. He saluted.

"At ease, Chief," she said. She had a clipboard in her hand. "I have here the paperwork for the dolphin named Tomas." She thrust the clipboard into his hands. "You have to put some signatures on it." She handed him a pen. He signed the forms, all of them medical records for the new dolphin they'd brought back. They were copies of the old forms that had been in the original Tomas's file, except now the information had been changed so that it matched the new dolphin's weight, measurements, and description. With a few strokes of Cory's pen, this Russian dolphin had taken on Tomas's identity completely. Dr. Morris had even removed Tomas's radio ID tag before giving them his body for the mission, and inserted it below the skin of the new dolphin as soon as it was brought back to the ship.

"This is the craziest thing I've ever done in my career," Dr. Morris said.

"Will your people play along?" Cory asked her.

"Anyone who knows what really happened here has no interest in seeing another dolphin hurt," she said. "They'll play along. And once we're back in the States, all the laws concerning the care and keeping of marine mammals will apply to this dolphin. He couldn't be put down even if the truth came out."

"But the truth won't come out," said Cory. He turned to the SEAL lieutenant. "Right, LT?"

"What truth?" the lieutenant said. All his guys leaned in to listen. "All I know is the dolphin team saved our mission, and that's all I'll say to anyone who asks. All any of us will say, right?" He turned to his team.

"Hooyah!" the SEALs answered in unison.

Cory turned back to the doctor. "How's Skunk doing?"

"See for yourself," she said. "Looks like he's making friends."

Cory walked over to Tomas's old tank, where the new Tomas had been placed. Skunk was kneeling on the small platform hanging over its side and he had a bucket of fish open next to him. The dolphin was watching him, trying to figure out what each of Skunk's hand gestures meant, what it needed to do to get a fish. Sometimes it was a barrel roll. Sometimes it was simply floating on its back so Skunk could examine its underside — an important maneuver to help with medical exams — and sometimes, the dolphin had no idea what Skunk wanted, so it would just flick its snout and splash Skunk across the face with salt water. It made Skunk laugh every time.

"You'd think you two had known each other for years," Cory said.

"We have," said Skunk. "Remember? From now on, this is Tomas."

Cory nodded, understanding. If they all believed the lie, even though they knew it wasn't true, it could, in a way, become true. It was a lie that saved a life. Cory had never thought a lie could be beautiful before, but in the midst of so much death, perhaps, together, he and the Navy SEALs and the dolphin team and these few brilliant dolphins had invented something new: a beautiful lie.

"How'd you get Preeti to go along?" Cory asked him.

"It was easier than I thought," Skunk said. "I just told her the truth."

"The truth?"

"I told her we couldn't do it without her because she was the best." Skunk shrugged. "Better than me and you, anyway."

Cory smirked. He looked across the cargo hold at Preeti and her dolphin, and he figured Skunk was right. He didn't mind. If this program had a future, she was it. She was tough, smart, and she'd proven that she'd do anything for her team.

He'd be glad to recommend her for his job. He hoped Commander Jackson would let him, because he knew he couldn't stay in the program any longer. After all he'd been through, all he'd put Kaj through, he didn't have another mission in him. He was no leader.

He was just a guy who cared about dolphins. He wanted to find a way to spend the rest of his days working on their behalf. Dolphins had served him well. It was time for him to serve them.

The new Tomas swam circles in his tank, splashing the edges as he got to know his strange new home, confused, perhaps, but learning.

Or, perhaps the dolphin understood the situation perfectly and was splashing for the simple joy of splashing, splashing simply because it could. Simply because it was alive.

AUTHOR'S NOTE

The books in the Tides of War series are works of fiction, but they are (loosely!) based on real programs and events.

There really is a US Navy Marine Mammal Program, based in San Diego, and until the 1990s, the program was classified. Over the years the navy has worked with a variety of marine mammals, including killer whales, pilot whales, beluga whales, and several types of seal and sea lion. Today, the navy works primarily with bottlenose dolphins and California sea lions to guard ships in port, recover equipment from the seafloor, and locate undersea mines.

In fact, according to the navy's statements, one rubber boat, one trained marine mammal, and two dolphin handlers can replace an entire navy vessel loaded with divers and doctors, expensive search equipment, and tons of fuel.

There is no such system as the Mark 6D team that I wrote about in this book. That was pure fantasy. There are, in realty, only five marine mammal systems — called MK 4, MK 5, MK 6, MK 7, and MK 8 — which use dolphins and sea lions to perform different tasks. Some animals will be used in more than one "Mark" system, depending on the need, but officially, none of them would be sent on combat missions with Navy SEALs. Dolphins would probably make lousy infantry soldiers . . . They have no way to know who is friend and who is foe. In my interviews, I learned of at least one Navy SEAL who was injured during training by one of our dolphins. They do their jobs well, but they do not make judgments about who is the enemy. That is an entirely human decision.

The dolphins and sea lions in the navy are given the same quality of care as dolphins in aquariums around the country, and the navy follows the same rules and guidelines for their care as any civilian institution. Research with these marine mammals has led to the publication of countless scientific papers and produced a variety of insights and discoveries about dolphins that are of immeasurable value to marine biologists.

But since the program's founding in 1960, there have been concerns about the treatment of the animals and the morality of using dolphins for military purposes. There is a lively debate about whether or not it is appropriate to keep dolphins in captivity and to use them for military or even entertainment purposes.

Dolphins are social creatures and need one another's company to survive. They communicate and remember and, from what we can tell, have rich and complex minds. We have learned a great deal from the dolphins we have studied in water parks, aquariums, and in the navy. The knowledge we have gained from them has allowed humans to find new ways to protect dolphins in the wild. But whether or not these programs should continue is a subject worthy of much more discussion, and there is no easy answer.

We have a long way to go toward responsible stewardship of our oceans and all the creatures in it, but I believe dolphins can be excellent partners in that effort, if they are treated with wisdom, generosity, and respect. The debate continues to this day, although the navy has announced that they will begin replacing the marine mammals with robots starting in 2017.

Another fact I used for inspiration for this story is the annexation of Crimea.

Russian-backed separatists did seize the Crimean peninsula in the late winter of 2014, and one of their first priorities was to secure control of the naval base at Sevastopol, where the Russian dolphin program was located. Hard facts are difficult to come by, as everyone involved denies being involved, but there is strong evidence to suggest that the Russian trained dolphins really were equipped with "kill darts" for "swimmer nullification." Of course, these are only rumors, and rumors often prove untrue.

In response to the annexation of Crimea, the US did deploy some of our dolphins to the Black Sea, although the details of this mission — which was publicly called a training exercise — are not known.

Those facts and rumors were the jumping off point for the adventure story you just read, but I made a lot of things up. Everything in this story is possible, but that does not mean that it is at all plausible or likely.

It is unlikely the US would have ordered a covert mission on shore into Crimea, or would have taken an active role in rescuing Ukrainian warships. It is unlikely that someone of Cory's rank and rating would have been able to do what he did in this story, or would have been in charge of the operation with so little supervision and also unlikely that he would have gotten away with his crazy plan.

To learn more about the real Marine Mammal Program, as well as the use and care of its dolphins and other sea mammals, you can visit the navy's Space and Naval Warfare Systems page: www.public.navy.mil /spawar/Pacific/71500/Pages/default.aspx.

Or you can explore the recent inside look the navy gave CNN, which includes videos of the dolphins at work: www.cnn.com/2011/US/07/31/marine.mammals .program/index.html.

PBS produced a brief timeline of the history of the navy dolphin program as well: www.pbs.org/wgbh /pages/frontline/shows/whales/etc/navycron.html.

To understand the history of human-dolphins relationships, the basic biology and training of dolphins, and the debate surrounding dolphins kept in captivity, I relied heavily on book *The Dolphin Mirror: Exploring Dolphin Minds and Saving Dolphin Lives* by Diana Reiss (Mariner Books), as well as *Dolphins in the Navy (America's Animal Soldiers)* by Meish Goldish (Bearport Publishing).

To learn more about the Navy SEALs, that elite fighting force, and get an inside look at how these brave men train, how they think, and how they operate around the globe, you could read *I Am a SEAL Team Six Warrior: Memoirs of an American Soldier* by Howard E. Wasdin and Stephen Templin (St. Martin's Griffin).

Any and all errors in this book are entirely my own, while most everything I got right I owe to the work and wisdom of others. I would especially like to thank my pal DMAC for giving me some great details and clearing up some confusion about the workings of the SEAL teams just when I needed it.

Thanks, too, to Nick Eliopulos, my friend and editor, for being such a fun partner in the creation of this series. And of course, I'm grateful to the rest of the Scholastic team, from the talented copy editors who make me seem smarter than I am, to the Book Fairs and Book Clubs staff, and the rest of the editorial, marketing, art, and publicity departments, who work night and day to get the right book to the right kid at the right time.

I'm also grateful for all the men and women who serve this country in the United States Navy, for the work they do, the skill with which they do it, and the risks so many of them take about which we will never know. While many of their triumphs and their defeats remain top secret, my admiration need not. As I've said before, to all the sailors and SEALs out there, as well as the civilians who work alongside them: Hooyah!

01:
SIR, NO, SIR

OUR helicopter flew over the edge of the great expanse of Arctic ice and came in low across the blue-green water of the Chukchi Sea.

"Fifteen minutes, sir," the crew chief told me through the intercom in my headset. We wouldn't be able to hear each other at all over the roar of the rotor blades and the wind if it weren't for the intercom, and even then I had trouble hearing him. Had he just called me *sir*?

"I'm not an officer," I told him.

"What's that, sir?"

"I said I'm not an officer," I repeated over the static of the mic. "You don't need to call me *sir*."

The crew chief gave me a funny look, like why would I object to being called *sir*. It was just one of those things that civilians usually didn't understand. The whole crew of the helicopter was made up of civilians and so was the crew of the ship we were heading to. Only two other members of my team were in the military, and none of us were officers. Officers were the managers and bosses, and even the most senior enlisted sailor had to call even the youngest, most inexperienced officer *sir*.

It was amazing how well those three letters could be used by a salty sea-dog enlisted man to call some young lieutenant a moron without the officer ever realizing it. Like "Yes, *sir*, the water is very blue today, *sir*," or "No, *sir*, I don't think it's a good idea to juggle with live hand grenades, *sir*."

I wasn't much of a fan of officers.

I'd joined the navy right out of high school and

worked my way up the ranks of enlisted personnel over the last few years to become a petty officer second class, rated as a Marine Mammal Systems operator, which meant I helped train, handle, care for, and document the work of the navy's dolphins and sea lions. I was proud of the hard work it had taken to become one of the best handlers in the navy's arsenal, so I didn't want this helicopter crewman from the Research Vessel *Buzz Aldrin* thinking I was some paper-pushing *officer*. I worked for a living.

But instead of telling him all that over the static of the intercom and the whomp of the helicopter blades, I just gave him a smile and turned back to my sea lion in his crate.

"Hansel" was chocolate brown, with big black eyes as wide as a cow's. He had little nubs for ears — which is why sea lions are also known as "eared seals" — and long, twitching whiskers at the end of his pointy snout. His snout also had a patch of tan fur right on the end, which I thought made him look dignified, an illusion that he always undid by hopping back and forth on his front flippers and barking whenever I paid him any attention. He was, in truth, more like an eager puppy than a majestic creature of the sea — a seven-hundred-pound puppy with a bone-crushing bite. He was also an expert at playing fetch.

With my guidance, Hansel had recovered torpedoes dropped on the ocean floor during training exercises, the lost "black box" recording device from a crashed airplane's cockpit five hundred feet below the ocean's surface, and an admiral's cell phone, which he had dropped off the side of a navy destroyer while yelling at some unfortunate junior officer.

Now we'd been sent to the Arctic Circle to fetch some expensive research equipment that had fallen through a crack in the ice sheet. I didn't know a lot about the mission yet, just that the civilian research ship had requested us, that they were funded by the navy, and that the mission had some kind of strategic importance to the United States.

"The Russian military is operating in the area," my commander had told me before I left Naval Base Point

Loma in San Diego. "But we do not expect any inter-ference from them. They've got their own oil and natural gas operations up there, and as long as we don't get in their way, they won't get in ours. Your primary dangers are going to be the cold — the water up there is far colder than what our sea lions are used to — and natural predators. Orcas feed off the local seal and wal-rus population, and this time of year, the polar bears are actively hunting. They eat seals and sea lions, too. You'll have to remain alert."

"Aye aye, *sir*," I told the commander, jabbing that *sir* in like a blade. As if I didn't know that the Arctic was cold or that killer whales and polar bears ate sea lions. I'd been working with Hansel for almost two years and read all the research about sea lions that I could get my hands on. I also had a subscription to *National Geographic*. Just because I didn't have a col-lege degree didn't mean I was a dummy.

In the cargo helicopter with me, I had the pieces to construct a large onboard cage for Hansel, a special warming vest the navy had invented for cold-water operations, and enough restaurant-quality fish to last my sea lion a week. I had all the equipment I'd need for the operation, and enough medical supplies to treat Hansel for anything from the sniffles to a heart attack.

I also had Dr. Morris, a civilian veterinarian who'd been with the program for ages, to actually provide Hansel's medical care, and two Marine Mammal technicians. Together, my people, my sea lion, the equipment, and I made up what we called the MK 5 System — "QuickFind" for short. We traveled with everything we needed, and we were prepared for anything the Arctic could throw at us.

At least, that's what I thought.

Until everything went wrong.

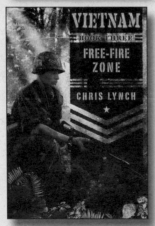
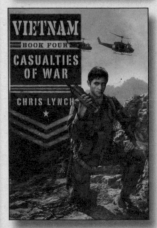

THE STUNNING ADVENTURE
FROM BESTSELLING AUTHOR
RICK RIORDAN

Available in print and eBook editions

www.the39clues.com